Jared Sparks, Benjamin Franklin

The Autobiography of Benjamin Franklin

Published verbatim from the original Manuscript

Jared Sparks, Benjamin Franklin

The Autobiography of Benjamin Franklin
Published verbatim from the original Manuscript

ISBN/EAN: 9783337119188

Printed in Europe, USA, Canada, Australia, Japan

Cover: Foto ©Raphael Reischuk / pixelio.de

More available books at **www.hansebooks.com**

THE

AUTOBIOGRAPHY

OF

BENJAMIN FRANKLIN.

PUBLISHED VERBATIM FROM THE ORIGINAL MANUSCRIPT,

BY HIS GRANDSON,

WILLIAM TEMPLE FRANKLIN,

EDITED BY

JARED SPARKS,

LONDON: GEORGE BELL & SONS, YORK STREET,
COVENT GARDEN.

1884.

ADVERTISEMENT.

Of Franklin's very entertaining and instructive Autobio·
graphy, there has, strange to say, been no authentic edition
of a popular character, yet published in this country. That
which has so often been presented to the British public,
in every variety of form, from the diminutive octo-decimo to
the imperial octavo, *is a mere translation from a French translation* (see Mr. Sparks' preface, annexed); and, however well
performed considering the circumstances, retains little of the
racy freshness and pleasing simplicity of the original. Besides
this, it differs in the narrative, is less comprehensive, and extends only to the year 1730 instead of to 1757.

The present Autobiography, which by way of distinction is
designated " the genuine," was first published from Franklin's manuscript, by his grandson, William Temple Franklin,
in 1817, in a selection of his works extending to six vols.
8vo. or three vols. 4to.; since which, only one edition in this
country has professed to follow it, and that is altogether
unfaithful, being a mere abridged compilation, written in
the third person by the compiler. Several complete editions,
however, have been published in America; the best of which,
by many degrees, is that recently edited by Jared Sparks,
one of the ablest biographers of the United States. Mr.
Sparks' edition, therefore, has been adopted as the basis of
the present.

In a future volume, it is intended to give the remainder
of the Biography, as completed by Mr. Sparks, together with
Franklin's Essays and a selection of his other works.

H. G. B.

York Street,
March, 1850.

PREFACE,

BY JARED SPARKS.

THERE is a curious circumstance connected with the first publication of the present Autobiography. Franklin began to write it, in England, as early as the year 1771, and from time to time he made such additions as his leisure would permit. While he was in France, as Minister Plenipotentiary from the United States, he showed a copy of it to some of his friends there, and one of them, M. Le Veillard, translated it into French. Not long after Dr. Franklin's death, this French translation appeared from the Paris press. It was then retranslated, by some unknown, but skilful hand, into English, and published in London; and this retranslation is the Life of Franklin which has usually been circulated in Great Britain and the United States, and of which numerous editions have been printed. And even to this day it continues to be read, and to be quoted by respectable writers, as if it were the author's original work; although the fact of its being a translation is expressly stated in the Preface to the first edition, and although many years have elapsed since the Autobiography was published from the original manuscript, by Franklin's grandson. In the present Volume it is printed from the genuine copy. Notes have been added to illustrate some parts, and the whole is divided into chapters, of suitable length, for the convenience of readers.

In writing the Continuation, it has been the Author's aim to follow out the plan of the Autobiography, by confining himself strictly to a narrative of the principal events and incidents in Franklin's life, as far as these could be ascertained from his writings, his public acts, and the testimony of his contemporaries. In executing this task, he has had access to a large mass of papers left by Franklin, including his correspondence with many persons in various parts of the world, and also to copious materials, of much value, procured in England, France, and the United States, all of which were for several years in his possession, while he was preparing for the press a new and complete edition of Franklin's Works. As he has spared no pains in his researches, or in his endeavours to make their results useful to the public, he trusts that his efforts have not been wholly without success, and that they will be regarded as having added something to the tribute justly due to the memory of the philosopher, statesman, and philanthropist, whose fame is an honour not more to the land of his birth, than to the age in which he lived.

JARED SPARKS.

CONTENTS.

THE

AUTOBIOGRAPHY*

OF

BENJAMIN FRANKLIN.

CHAPTER I.

I HAVE ever had a pleasure in obtaining any little anecdotes of my ancestors. You may remember the inquiries I
made among the remains of my relations when you were with
me in England, and the journey I undertook for that purpose.
Imagining it may be equally agreeable to you to learn the
circumstances of *my* life, many of which you are unacquainted
with; and expecting the enjoyment of a few weeks' uninter-
rupted leisure, I sit down to write them. Besides, there are
some other inducements that excite me to this undertaking.
From the poverty and obscurity in which I was born, and in
which I passed my earliest years, I have raised myself to a
state of affluence and some degree of celebrity in the world.
As constant good fortune has accompanied me even to an
advanced period of life, my posterity will perhaps be desirous
of learning the means which I employed, and which, thanks
to Providence, so well succeeded with me. They may also
deem them fit to be imitated, should any of them find themselves in similar circumstances.

This good fortune, when I reflect on it (which is frequently
the case), has induced me sometimes to say, that, if it were
left to my choice, I should have no objection to go over the
same life from its beginning to the end; requesting only the
advantage authors have of correcting in a second edition the
faults of the first. So would I also wish to change some
incidents of it, for others more favourable. Notwithstanding,
if this condition was denied, I should still accept the offer of
recommencing the same life. But as this repetition is not

* The first part of the Autobiography, constituting the first five
Chapters of this edition, was written in the form of a letter to his son,
William Franklin, then Governor of New Jersey. It was begun while
the author was on a visit to the family of Dr. Shipley, Bishop of St.
Asaph, at Twyford, in the year 1771.—ED.

to be expected, that which resembles most living one's life over again, seems to be to recall all the circumstances of it, and, to render this remembrance more durable, to record them in writing.

In thus employing myself, I shall yield to the inclination so natural to old men, of talking of themselves and their own actions; and I shall indulge it without being tiresome to those who, from respect to my age, might conceive themselves obliged to listen to me, since they will be always free to read me or not. And, lastly (I may as well confess it, as the denial of it would be believed by nobody), I shall, perhaps, not a little gratify my own vanity. Indeed, I never heard or saw the introductory words, "Without vanity I may say," &c., but some vain thing immediately followed. Most people dislike vanity in others, whatever share they have of it themselves; but I give it fair quarter wherever I meet with it, being persuaded that it is often productive of good to the possessor, and to others who are within his sphere of action; and therefore, in many cases, it would not be altogether absurd, if a man were to thank God for his *vanity* among the other comforts of life.

And now I speak of thanking God, I desire, with all humility, to acknowledge that I attribute the mentioned happiness of my past life to His divine providence, which led me to the means I used, and gave the success. My belief of this induces me to *hope*, though I must not *presume*, that the same goodness will still be exercised towards me in continuing that happiness, or enabling me to bear a fatal reverse, which I may experience as others have done; the complexion of my future fortune being known to Him only in whose power it is to bless us, even in our afflictions.

Some notes, which one of my uncles, who had the same curiosity in collecting family anecdotes, once put into my hands, furnished me with several particulars relative to our ancestors. From these notes I learned, that they lived in the same village, Ecton, in Northamptonshire, on a freehold of about thirty acres, for at least three hundred years, and how much longer could not be ascertained.*

* Perhaps from the time, when the name of Franklin, which before was the name of an order of people, was assumed by them for a *surname*, when others took surnames all over the kingdom.
As a proof that Franklin was anciently the common name of an order or rank in England, see Judge Fortescue, *De laudibus Legum Angliæ,*

This small estate would not have sufficed for their mainte-
nance without the business of a smith, which had continued
in the family down to my uncle's time, the eldest son being
always brought up to that employment; a custom which he
and my father followed with regard to their eldest sons. When
I searched the registers at Ecton, I found an account of their
marriages and burials from the year 1555 only, as the registers
kept did not commence previous thereto. I, however, learned
from it that I was the youngest son of the youngest son for
five generations back. My grandfather, Thomas, who was born
in 1598, lived at Ecton till he was too old to continue his
business, when he retired to Banbury, in Oxfordshire, to the
house of his son John, with whom my father served an apprenticeship. There my uncle died, and lies buried. We saw his
gravestone in 1758. His eldest son Thomas lived in the house
at Ecton, and left it, with the land, to his only daughter, who,
with her husband, one Fisher, of Wellingborough, sold it to
Mr. Isted, now lord of the manor there. My grandfather had
four sons, who grew up; viz., Thomas, John, Benjamin, and
Josiah. Being at a distance from my papers, I will give you
what account I can of them from memory; and if my papers
are not lost in my absence, you will find among them many
more particulars.

Thomas, my eldest uncle, was bred a smith under his father,
but, being ingenious, and encouraged in learning, as all his
written about the year 1412, in which is the following passage, to show
that good juries might easily be formed in any part of England.

"Moreover, the same country is so filled and replenished with landed
menne, that therein so small a Thorpe cannot be found wherein
dwelleth not a knight, an esquire, or such a householder, as is there
commonly called a *Franklin*, enriched with great possessions; and also
other freeholders, and many yeomen able for their livelihoods to make
a jury in form aforementioned."—*Old Translation.*

Chaucer, too, calls his Country Gentleman a *Franklin*, and, after
describing his good housekeeping, thus characterizes him.

"This worthy Franklin bore a purse of silk,
Fixed to his girdle, white as morning milk.
Knight of the Shire, first Justice at th' Assize,
To help the poor, the doubtful to advise.
In all employments, generous, just, he proved;
Renowned for courtesy, by all beloved."

Again—
——"A spacious court they see,
Both plain and pleasant to be walked in,
Where them does meet a Franklin fair and free."
SPENSER'S *Faery Queen.*

B 2

brothers were by an Esquire Palmer, then the principal inhabitant of that parish, he qualified himself for the bar, and became a considerable man in the county; was chief mover of all public-spirited enterprises for the county or town of Northampton, as well as of his own village, of which many instances were related of him; and he was much taken notice of and patronised by Lord Halifax. He died in 1702, the 6th of January, four years, to a day, before I was born. The recital which some elderly persons made to us of his character, I remember struck you as something extraordinary, from its similarity with what you knew of me. " Had he died," said you, " four years later, on the same day, one might have supposed a transmigration."

John, my next uncle, was bred a dyer, I believe of wool. Benjamin was bred a silk dyer, serving an apprenticeship in London. He was an ingenious man. I remember, when I was a boy, he came to my father's in Boston, and resided in the house with us for several years. There was always a particular affection between my father and him, and I was his godson. He lived to a great age. He left behind him two quarto volumes of manuscript, of his own poetry, consisting of fugitive pieces addressed to his friends.* He had invented a short-hand of his own, which he taught me; but, not having practised it, I have now forgotten it. He was very pious, and an assiduous attendant at the sermons of the best preachers, which he reduced to writing according to his method, and had thus collected several volumes of them.

He was also a good deal of a politician; too much so, perhaps, for his station. There fell lately into my hands, in London, a collection he had made of all the principal political pamphlets relating to public affairs, from the year 1641 to 1717. Many of the volumes are wanting, as appears by their numbering; but there still remain eight volumes in folio, and twenty in quarto and in octavo. A dealer in old books had met with them, and, knowing me by name, having bought books of him, he brought them to me. It would appear that my uncle must have left them here, when he went to America, which was about fifty years ago. I found several of his notes in the margins. His grandson, Samuel Franklin, is still living in Boston.†

* These two volumes have been preserved, and are now before me. They belong to Mrs. Emmons, of Boston, great-grand-daughter of Benjamin Franklin, their author.—ED.
† This grandson of Benjamin Franklin followed the trade of his

Our humble family early embraced the reformed religion. Our forefathers continued Protestants through the reign of Mary, when they were sometimes in danger of persecution, on account of their zeal against popery. They had an English Bible, and to conceal it and place it in safety, it was fastened open with tapes, under and within the cover of a joint stool. When my great-grandfather wished to read it to his family, he placed the joint stool on his knees, and then turned over the leaves under the tapes. One of the children stood at the door to give notice if he saw the apparitor coming, who was an officer of the spiritual court. In that case the stool was turned down again upon its feet, when the Bible remained concealed under it as before. This anecdote I had from uncle Benjamin. The family continued all of the church of England till about the end of Charles the Second's reign, when some of the ministers that had been outed for their non-conformity, holding conventicles in Northamptonshire, my uncle Benjamin and my father Josiah adhered to them, and so continued all their lives. The rest of the family remained with the Episcopal church.

My father married young, and carried his wife, with three children, to New England, about 1685. The conventicles being at that time forbidden by law, and frequently disturbed in the meetings, some considerable men of his acquaintances determined to go to that country, and he was prevailed with to accompany them thither, where they expected to enjoy the exercise of their religion with freedom. By the same wife my father had four children more born there, and by a second, ten others,—in all seventeen; of whom I remember to have seen thirteen sitting together at his table; who all grew up to years of maturity, and were married. I was the youngest son, and the youngest of all the children except two daughters.

father, which was that of a cutler. On the father's sign, suspended over the shop door, was painted a crown, with his name, " Samuel Franklin, from London." It had also some of the implements of his trade. This sign was retained by Samuel Franklin the younger. At the beginning of the Revolution, the " Sons of Liberty" took offence at this crown, and demanded the removal of the sign; but they finally contented themselves with daubing a coat of paint over the crown, leaving " Samuel Franklin, from London," and the implements of cutlery. Time gradually wore off the paint from the crown, so as to make it faintly visible; and Mather Byles, who was as noted for his loyalty as for his puns, used to lament to Mrs. Franklin, that she should live at the sign of the *half-crown.*—ED.

I was born in Boston, in New England.* My mother, the second wife of my father, was Abiah Folger, daughter of Peter Folger, one of the first settlers of New England; of whom honourable mention is made by Cotton Mather, in his ecclesiastical history of that country, entitled *Magnalia Christi Americana*, as "a godly and learned Englishman," if I remember the words rightly. I was informed he wrote several small occasional works, but only one of them was printed, which I remember to have seen several years since. It was written in 1675. It was in familiar verse, according to the taste of the times and people; and addressed to the government there. It asserts the liberty of conscience in behalf of the Anabaptists, the Quakers, and other sectaries, that had been persecuted. He attributes to this persecution the Indian wars, and other calamities that had befallen the country; regarding them as so many judgments of God to punish so heinous an offence, and exhorting the repeal of those laws, so contrary to charity. This piece appeared to me as written with manly freedom, and a pleasing simplicity. The six last lines I remember, but have forgotten the preceding ones of the stanza; the purport of them was, that his censures proceeded from good will, and therefore he would be known to be the author:—

> "Because to be a libeller
>   I hate it with my heart.
> From Sherbon Town† where now I dwell,
>   My name I do put here;
> Without offence your real friend,
>   It is Peter Folger."‡

My elder brothers were all put apprentices to different trades. I was put to the grammar school at eight years of

* He was born January 6th, 1706, Old Style, being Sunday, and the same as January 17th, New Style, which his biographers have usually mentioned as the day of his birth. By the records of the old South Church in Boston, to which his father and mother belonged, it appears that he was baptized the same day. In the old public Register of Births, still preserved in the Mayor's office in Boston, his birth is recorded under the date of January 6th, 1706. At this time his father occupied a house in Milk Street, opposite to the Old South Church, but he removed shortly afterwards to a house at the corner of Hanover and Union Streets, where it is believed he resided the remainder of his life, and where the son passed his early years.—ED.

† In the island of Nantucket.

‡ The poem, if such it may be called, of which these are the closing lines, extends through fourteen pages of a duodecimo pamphlet, entitled, "*A Looking-Glass for the Times; or the former Spirit of New England revived in this generation;* by PETER FOLGER." It is dated at the

age; my father intending to devote me, as the tithe of his sons, to the service of the church. My early readiness in learning to read, which must have been very early, as I do not remember when I could not read, and the opinion of all his friends that I should certainly make a good scholar, encouraged him in this purpose of his. My uncle Benjamin, too, approved of it, and proposed to give me his short-hand volumes of sermons, to set up with, if I would learn his short-hand. I continued, however, at the grammar school rather less than a year, though in that time I had risen gradually from the middle of the class of that year to be at the head of the same class, and was removed into the next class, whence I was to be placed in the third at the end of the year.

But my father, burdened with a numerous family, was unable, without inconvenience, to support the expense of a college education. Considering, moreover, as he said to one of his friends, in my presence, the little encouragement that line of life afforded to those educated for it, he gave up his first intentions, took me from the grammar school, and sent me to a school for writing and arithmetic, kept by a then famous man, Mr. George Brownwell. He was a skilful master, and successful in his profession, employing the mildest and most encouraging methods. Under him I learned to write a good hand pretty soon; but I failed entirely in arithmetic. At ten years old I was taken to help my father in his business, which was that of a tallow-chandler and soap-boiler; a business to which he was not bred, but had assumed on his arrival in New England, because he found that his dyeing trade, being in little request, would not maintain his family. Accordingly, I was employed in cutting wicks for the candles, filling the moulds for cast candles, attending the shop, going of errands, &c.

I disliked the trade, and had a strong inclination to go to sea; but my father declared against it. But, residing near

end, "April 23rd, 1676." The lines which immediately precede those quoted by Dr. Franklin, and which are necessary to complete the sentiment intended to be conveyed by the author, are the following :—

"I am for peace and not for war,
   And that's the reason why
I write more plain than some men do,
   That use to daub and lie.
But I shall cease, and set my name
   To what I here insert,
Because to be a libeller," &c.—ED.

the water, I was much in it and on it. I learned to swim well
and to manage boats; and, when embarked with other boys,
I was commonly allowed to govern, especially in any case of
difficulty; and upon other occasions I was generally the
leader among the boys, and sometimes led them into scrapes,
of which I will mention one instance, as it shows an early
projecting public spirit, though not then justly conducted.
There was a salt marsh, which bounded part of the millpond
on the edge of which, at high water, we used to stand to fish
for minnows. By much trampling we had made it a mere
quagmire. My proposal was to build a wharf there for us to
stand upon, and I shewed my comrades a large heap of
stones, which were intended for a new house near the marsh,
and which would very well suit our purpose. Accordingly in
the evening, when the workmen were gone home, I assembled
a number of my playfellows, and we worked diligently like
so many emmets, sometimes two or three to a stone, till we
brought them all to make our little wharf. The next morning
the workmen were surprised at missing the stones, which
had formed our wharf. Inquiry was made after the authors
of this transfer; we were discovered, complained of, and
corrected by our fathers; and, though I demonstrated the
utility of our work, mine convinced me, that that which
was not honest, could not be truly useful.

I suppose you may like to know what kind of a man my
father was. He had an excellent constitution, was of a middle
stature, well set, and very strong. He could draw prettily,
and was skilled a little in music. His voice was sonorous
and agreeable, so that when he played on his violin, and sung
withal, as he was accustomed to do after the business of the
day was over, it was extremely agreeable to hear. He had
some knowledge of mechanics, and on occasion was very
handy with other tradesmen's tools. But his great excellence
was his sound understanding, and his solid judgment in
prudential matters, both in private and public affairs. It is
true he was never employed in the latter, the numerous family
he had to educate, and the straitness of his circumstances,
keeping him close to his trade; but I remember well his being
frequently visited by leading men, who consulted him for his
opinion in public affairs, and those of the church he belonged
to; and who showed a great respect for his judgment and
advice.

He was also much consulted by private persons about their
affairs, when any difficulty occurred, and frequently chosen an

arbitrator between contending parties.   At his table he liked
to have, as often as he could, some sensible friend or neighbour to converse with, and always took care to start some
ingenious or useful topic for discourse, which might tend to
improve the minds of his children.   By this means he turned
our attention to what was good, just, and prudent, in the
conduct of life; and little or no notice was ever taken of what
related to the victuals on the table; whether it was well or ill
dressed, in or out of season, of good or bad flavour, preferable
or inferior to this or that other thing of the kind; so that I
was brought up in such a perfect inattention to those matters
as to be quite indifferent what kind of food was set before me.
Indeed, I am so unobservant of it, that to this day I can
scarce tell a few hours after dinner of what dishes it consisted.   This has been a great convenience to me in travelling,
where my companions have been sometimes very unhappy for
want of a suitable gratification of their more delicate, because
better instructed, tastes and appetites.

My mother had likewise an excellent constitution; she
suckled all her ten children.   I never knew either my father
or mother to have any sickness, but that of which they died;
he at eighty-nine, and she at eighty-five years of age.   They
lie buried together at Boston, where I some years since
placed a marble over their grave, with this inscription:

JOSIAH FRANKLIN
and
ABIAH his wife,
Lie here interred.
They lived lovingly together in wedlock,
Fifty-five years;
And without an estate or any gainful employment,
By constant labour, and honest industry,
(With God's blessing,)
Maintained a large family comfortably;
And brought up thirteen children and seven grandchildren
Reputably.
From this instance, Reader,
Be encouraged to diligence in thy calling,
And distrust not Providence.
He was a pious and prudent man,
She a discreet and virtuous woman.
Their youngest son,
In filial regard to their memory,
Places this stone.
J. F. born 1655; died 1744.   Æt. 89.
A. F. born 1667; died 1752.   Æt. 85.*

* The marble stone on which this inscription was engraved, having

By my rambling digressions, I perceive myself to be grown old. I used to write more methodically. But one does not dress for private company, as for a public ball. Perhaps it is only negligence.

To return; I continued thus employed in my father's business for two years, that is, till I was twelve years old; and, my brother John, who was bred to that business, having left my father, married, and set up for himself at Rhode Island, there was every appearance that I was destined to supply his place, and become a tallow-chandler. But my dislike to the trade continuing, my father had apprehensions

become decayed, and the inscription itself defaced by time, a more durable monument has been erected over the graves of the father and mother of Franklin. The suggestion was first made at a meeting of the building committee of the Bunker Hill Monument Association, in the autumn of 1826, and it met with universal approbation. A committee of management was organized, and an amount of money adequate to the object was soon contributed by the voluntary subscriptions of a large number of the citizens of Boston. The corner-stone was laid on the 15th of June, 1827, and an address appropriate to the occasion was pronounced by General Henry A. S. Dearborn.

The monument is an obelisk of granite, twenty-one feet high, which rests on a square base, measuring seven feet on each side, and two feet in height. The obelisk is composed of five massive blocks of granite placed one above another. On one side is the name of Franklin in large bronze letters, and a little below is a tablet of bronze, thirty-two inches long and sixteen wide, sunk into the stone. On this tablet is engraved Dr. Franklin's original inscription, as quoted in the text, and beneath it are the following lines:—

"The marble tablet,
Bearing the above inscription,
Having been dilapidated by the ravages of time,
A number of citizens,
Entertaining the most profound veneration
For the memory of the illustrious
Benjamin Franklin,
And desirous of reminding succeeding generations,
That he was born in Boston, A. D. MDCCVI,
Erected this
Obelisk
Over the graves of his parents.
MDCCCXXVII."

A silver plate was deposited under the corner-stone, with an inscription commemorative of the occasion; a part of which is as follows: "This Monument was erected over the Remains of the Parents of Benjamin Franklin by the Citizens of Boston, from Respect to the Private Character and Public Services of this Illustrious Patriot and Philosopher, and for the many Tokens of his affectionate Attachment to his native Town."—ED.

that, if he did not put me to one more agreeable, I should break loose and go to sea, as my brother Josiah had done, to his great vexation. In consequence, he took me to walk with him and see joiners, bricklayers, turners, braziers, &c., at their work, that he might observe my inclination, and endeavour to fix it on some trade or profession that would keep me on land. It has ever since been a pleasure to me to see good workmen handle their tools. And it has been often useful to me, to have learned so much by it, as to be able to do some trifling jobs in the house, when a workman was not at hand, and to construct little machines for my experiments, at the moment when the intention of making these was warm in my mind. My father determined at last for the cutler's trade, and placed me for some days on trial with Samuel, son to my uncle Benjamin, who was bred to that trade in London, and had just established himself in Boston. But the sum he exacted as a fee for my apprenticeship displeased my father, and I was taken home again.

From my infancy I was passionately fond of reading, and all the money that came into my hands was laid out in the purchasing of books. I was very fond of voyages. My first acquisition was Bunyan's works in separate little volumes; I afterwards sold them to enable me to buy R. Burton's *Historical Collections*. They were small chapmen's books,* and cheap; forty volumes in all. My father's little library consisted chiefly of books in polemic divinity, most of which I read. I have often regretted, that, at a time when I had such a thirst for knowledge, more proper books had not fallen in my way, since it was resolved I should not be bred to divinity. There was among them Plutarch's *Lives*, which I read abundantly, and I still think that time spent to great advantage. There was also a book of Defoe's, called *An Essay on Projects*, and another of Dr. Mather's, called *An Essay to do Good*, which perhaps gave me a turn of thinking, that had an influence on some of the principal future events of my life.

This bookish inclination at length determined my father to make me a printer, though he had already one son, James, of that profession. In 1717 my brother James returned from

* Commonly called "chap-books," a term applied to popular story books, which in former days used to be hawked about by chapmen, such as Tom Hickathrift, Jack the Giant Killer, &c. Burton's Histories were of rather a better class, and comprised "The English Hero, or, Sir Francis Drake Revived;" "Admirable Curiosities," &c., &c.

England with a press and letters, to set up his business in Boston. I liked it much better than that of my father, but still had a hankering for the sea. To prevent the apprehended effect of such an inclination, my father was impatient to have me bound to my brother. I stood out some time, but at last was persuaded, and signed the indenture, when I was yet but twelve years old. I was to serve an apprenticeship till I was twenty-one years of age, only I was to be allowed journeyman's wages during the last year. In a little time I made a great progress in the business, and became a useful hand to my brother. I now had access to better books. An acquaintance with the apprentices of booksellers enabled me sometimes to borrow a small one, which I was careful to return soon, and clean. Often I sat up in my chamber reading the greatest part of the night, when the book was borrowed in the evening and to be returned in the morning, lest it should be found missing.

After some time a merchant, an ingenious, sensible man, Mr. Matthew Adams, who had a pretty collection of books, frequented our printing office, took notice of me, and invited me to see his library, and very kindly proposed to lend me such books as I chose to read. I now took a strong inclination for poetry, and wrote some little pieces. My brother, supposing it might turn to account, encouraged me, and induced me to compose two occasional ballads. One was called *The Light-House Tragedy*, and contained an account of the shipwreck of Captain Worthilake with his two daughters; the other was a sailor's song, on the taking of the famous *Teach*, or *Blackbeard*, the pirate. They were wretched stuff, in street-ballad style; and when they were printed, my brother sent me about the town to sell them. The first sold prodigiously, the event being recent, and having made a great noise. This success flattered my vanity; but my father discouraged me by criticizing my performances, and telling me versemakers were generally beggars. Thus I escaped being a poet, and probably a very bad one; but, as prose writing has been of great use to me in the course of my life, and was a principal means of my advancement, I shall tell you how in such a situation I acquired what little ability I may be supposed to have in that way.

There was another bookish lad in the town, John Collins by name, with whom I was intimately acquainted. We sometimes disputed, and very fond we were of argument, and very desirous of confuting one another; which disputatious turn, by the way, is apt to become a very bad habit, making people often extremely disagreeable in company, by the contradiction that is necessary to bring it into practice; and thence, besides souring and spoiling the conversation, it is productive of disgusts, and perhaps enmities, with those who may have occasion for friendship. I had caught this by reading my father's books of dispute on religion. Persons of good sense, I have since observed, seldom fall into it, except lawyers, university men, and generally men of all sorts, who have been bred at Edinburgh.

A question was once, somehow or other, started between Collins and me, on the propriety of educating the female sex in learning, and their abilities for study. He was of opinion that it was improper, and that they were naturally unequal to it. I took the contrary side, perhaps a little for dispute's sake. He was naturally more eloquent, having a greater plenty of words, and sometimes, as I thought, I was vanquished more by his fluency than by the strength of his reasons. As we parted without settling the point, and were not to see one another again for some time, I sat down to put my arguments in writing, which I copied fair and sent to him. He answered and I replied. Three or four letters on a side had passed, when my father happened to find my papers, and read them. Without entering into the subject in dispute, he took occasion to talk to me about my manner of writing; observed that though I had the advantage of my antagonist in correct spelling and pointing (which he attributed to the printing-house), I fell far short in elegance of expression, in method, and in perspicuity, of which he convinced me by several instances. I saw the justice of his remarks, and thence grew more attentive to my manner of writing, and determined to endeavour to improve my style.

About this time I met with an odd volume of the *Spectator*. I had never before seen any of them. I bought it, read it over and over, and was much delighted with it. I thought the writing excellent, and wished if possible to imitate it. With that view I took some of the papers, and making short hints of the sentiments in each sentence, laid them by a few days, and then, without looking at the book, tried to complete the papers again, by expressing each hinted sentiment at length, and as fully as it had been expressed before, in

any suitable words that should occur to me. Then I com-
pared my Spectator with the original, discovered some of my
faults, and corrected them. But I found I wanted a stock of
words, or a readiness in recollecting and using them, which I
thought I should have acquired before that time, if I had
gone on making verses; since the continual search for words
of the same import, but of different length to suit the measure, or of different sound for the rhyme, would have laid
me under a constant necessity of searching for variety, and
also have tended to fix that variety in my mind, and make
me master of it. Therefore I took some of the tales in the
Spectator, and turned them into verse; and, after a time,
when I had pretty well forgotten the prose, turned them back
again.

I also sometimes jumbled my collection of hints into confusion,
and after some weeks endeavoured to reduce them into the best
order before I began to form the full sentences and complete
the subject. This was to teach me method in the arrange-
ment of the thoughts. By comparing my work with the
original, I discovered many faults, and corrected them; but I
sometimes had the pleasure to fancy, that, in certain particulars of small consequence, I had been fortunate enough to
improve the method or the language, and this encouraged me
to think that I might in time come to be a tolerable English
writer, of which I was extremely ambitious. The time I
allotted for writing exercises, and for reading, was at night,
or before work began in the morning, or on Sundays, when I
contrived to be in the printing-house, avoiding as much as I
could the constant attendance at public worship, which my
father used to exact of me when I was under his care, and
which I still continued to consider a duty, though I could not
afford time to practise it.

When about sixteen years of age, I happened to meet with
a book, written by one Tryon, recommending a vegetable
diet. I determined to go into it. My brother, being yet
unmarried, did not keep house, but boarded himself and his
apprentices in another family. My refusing to eat flesh occasioned an inconvenience, and I was frequently chid for my
singularity. I made myself acquainted with Tryon's manner
of preparing some of his dishes, such as boiling potatoes or
rice, making hasty pudding and a few others, and then proposed to my brother, that if he would give me weekly half
the money he paid for my board, I would board myself. He

instantly agreed to it, and I presently found that I could save half what he paid me. This was an additional fund for buying of books; but I had another advantage in it. My brother and the rest going from the printing-house to their meals, I remained there alone, and despatching presently my light repast (which was often no more than a biscuit, or a slice of bread, a handful of raisins, or a tart from the pastry cook's, and a glass of water), had the rest of the time, till their return, for study; in which I made the greater progress from that greater clearness of head and quicker apprehension which generally attend temperance in eating and drinking. Now it was that (being on some occasion made ashamed of my ignorance in figures, which I had twice failed learning when at school,) I took Cocker's book on *Arithmetic*, and went through the whole by myself with the greatest ease. I also read Seller's and Sturny's book on *Navigation*, which made me acquainted with the little geometry it contains; but I never proceeded far in that science. I read about this time Locke *On Human Understanding*, and *The Art of Thinking* by Messrs. de Port-Royal.

While I was intent on improving my language, I met with an English grammar (I think it was Greenwood's), having at the end of it two little sketches on the Arts of Rhetoric and Logic, the latter finishing with a dispute in the Socratic method; and soon after I procured Xenophon's *Memorable Things of Socrates*, wherein there are many examples of the same method. I was charmed with it, adopted it, dropped my abrupt contradictions and positive argumentation, and put on the humble inquirer. And being then from reading Shaftesbury and Collins made a doubter, as I already was in many points of our religious doctrines, I found this method the safest for myself and very embarrassing to those against whom I used it; therefore I took delight in it, practised it continually, and grew very artful and expert in drawing people even of superior knowledge into concessions, the consequences of which they did not foresee, entangling them in difficulties out of which they could not extricate themselves, and so obtaining victories that neither myself nor my cause always deserved.

I continued this method some few years, but gradually left it, retaining only the habit of expressing myself in terms of modest diffidence, never using, when I advance anything that may possibly be disputed, the words *certainly*, **undoubtedly**, or any others that give the air of positiveness to an opinion; but rather say, *I conceive*, or *apprehend*, a thing to be so and so; *It appears to me*, or *I should not think it, so or so, for such and such reasons ;* or, *I imagine it to be so ;* or, *It is so, if I am not mistaken.* This habit, I believe, has been of great advantage to me when I have had occasion to inculcate my opinions and persuade men into measures that I have been from time to time engaged in promoting. And as the chief ends of conversation are to *inform* or to *be informed*, to *please* or to *persuade*, I wish well-meaning and sensible men would not lessen their power of doing good by a positive assuming manner, that seldom fails to disgust, tends to create opposition, and to defeat most of those purposes for which speech was given to us. In fact, if you wish to instruct others, a positive dogmatical manner in advancing your sentiments may occasion opposition, and prevent a candid attention. If you desire instruction and improvement from others, you should not at the same time express yourself fixed in your present opinions. Modest and sensible men, who do not love disputation, will leave you undisturbed in the possession of your errors. In adopting such a manner, you can seldom expect to please your hearers, or obtain the concurrence you desire. Pope judiciously observes,

> " Men must be taught, as if you taught them not,
> And things unknown proposed as things forgot."

He also recommends it to us,

> " To speak, though sure, with seeming diffidence."

And he might have joined with this line, that which he has coupled with another, I think, less properly,

> " For want of modesty is want of sense."

If you ask, Why less properly ? I must repeat the lines,

> " Immodest words admit of no defence,
> For want of modesty is want of sense."

Now, is not the *want of sense*, where a man is so unfortunate as to want it, some apology for his *want of modesty?* And would not the lines stand more justly thus ?

> " Immodest words admit *but* this defence,
> That want of modesty is want of sense."

This, however, I should submit to better judgments.

My brother had, in 1720 or 1721, begun to print a newspaper. It was the second that appeared in America, and was called the *New England Courant.* The only one before it was the *Boston News-Letter*. I remember his being dissuaded by some of his friends from the undertaking, as not likely to succeed, one newspaper being in their judgment enough for America.* At this time, 1771, there are not less than five-and-twenty. He went on, however, with the undertaking. I was employed to carry the papers to the customers, after having worked in composing the types and printing off the sheets.

He had some ingenious men among his friends, who amused themselves by writing little pieces for this paper, which gained it credit, and made it more in demand, and these gentlemen often visited us. Hearing their conversations, and their accounts of the approbation their papers were received with, I was excited to try my hand among them. But, being still a boy, and suspecting that my brother would object to printing anything of mine in his paper, if he knew it to be mine, I contrived to disguise my hand, and, writing an anonymous paper, I put it at night under the door of the printing-house. It was found in the morning, and communicated to his writing friends when they called in as usual. They read it, commented on it in my hearing, and I had the exquisite pleasure of finding it met with their approbation, and that, in their different guesses at the author, none were named but men of some character among us for learning and ingenuity. I suppose, that I was rather lucky in my judges, and that they were not really so very good as I then believed them to be. Encouraged however by this attempt, I wrote and sent in the same way to the press several other pieces, that were equally approved; and I kept my secret till all my fund of sense for such performances was exhausted, and then discovered it, when I began to be considered a little more by my brother's acquaintance.

* This was written from recollection, and it is not surprising, that, after the lapse of fifty years, the author's memory should have failed him in regard to a fact of small importance. The *New England Courant* was the *fourth* newspaper that appeared in America. The first number of the *Boston News-Letter* was published April 24th, 1704. This was the first newspaper in America. The *Boston Gazette* commenced December 21st, 1719; the *American Weekly Mercury*, at Philadelphia, December 22nd, 1719; the *New England Courant*, August 21st, 1721. Dr. Franklin's error of memory probably originated in the circumstance of his brother having been the printer of the *Boston Gazette*, when it was first established. This was the *second* newspaper published in America.—ED.

C

However, that did not quite please him, as he thought it tended to make me too vain. This might be one occasion of the differences we began to have about this time. Though a brother, he considered himself as my master, and me as his apprentice, and accordingly expected the same services from me as he would from another, while I thought he degraded me too much in some he required of me, who from a brother expected more indulgence. Our disputes were often brought before our father, and I fancy I was either generally in the right, or else a better pleader, because the judgment was generally in my favour. But my brother was passionate, and had often beaten me, which I took extremely amiss; and, thinking my apprenticeship very tedious, I was continually wishing for some opportunity of shortening it, which at length offered in a manner unexpected. Perhaps this harsh and tyrannical treatment of me might be a means of impressing me with the aversion to arbitrary power, that has stuck to me through my whole life.

One of the pieces in our newspaper on some political point, which I have now forgotten, gave offence to the Assembly. He was taken up, censured, and imprisoned for a month by the Speaker's warrant, I suppose because he would not discover the author. I too was taken up and examined before the Council; but, though I did not give them any satisfaction, they contented themselves with admonishing me, and dismissed me, considering me perhaps as an apprentice, who was bound to keep his master's secrets. During my brother's confinement, which I resented a good deal notwithstanding our private differences, I had the management of the paper; and I made bold to give our rulers some rubs in it, which my brother took very kindly, while others began to consider me in an unfavorable light, as a youth that had a turn for libelling and satire.

My brother's discharge was accompanied with an order, and a very odd one, that "*James Franklin* should no longer print the newspaper, called *The New England Courant.*" On a consultation held in our printing-office amongst his friends, what he should do in this conjuncture, it was proposed to elude the order by changing the name of the paper. But my brother, seeing inconveniences in this, came to a conclusion, as a better way, to let the paper in future be printed in the name of *Benjamin Franklin;* and in order to avoid the censure of the Assembly, that might fall on him, as still print-

‘ng it by his apprentice, he contrived and consented that my old indenture should be returned to me with a discharge on the back of it, to show in case of necessity; and, in order to secure to him the benefit of my service, I should sign new indentures for the remainder of my time, which were to be kept private. A very flimsy scheme it was; however, it was immediately executed, and the paper was printed accordingly, under my name, for several months*.

* The earlier numbers of the *New England Courant* were principally filled with original articles, in the form of essays, letters, and short paragraphs, written with considerable ability and wit, and touching with great freedom the vices and follies of the time. The weapon of satire was used with an unsparing hand. Neither the government nor the clergy escaped. Much caution was practised, however, in regard to individuals, and names were seldom introduced. There are some severe and humerous criticisms on the poets of the day, which may be classed with the best specimens of this kind of composition in the modern reviews. The humour sometimes degenerates into coarseness, and the phraseology is often harsh; but, bating these faults, the paper contains nothing, which in later times would have been deemed reprehensible. James Franklin, the editor and printer, was imprisoned on the general charge of having published passages "boldly reflecting on his Majesty's government and on the administration in this province, the ministry, churches, and college; and that tend to fill the readers' minds with vanity, to the dishonour of God and the disservice of good men." He was sentenced by a vote of the Assembly, without any specification of these offensive passages, or any trial before a court of justice.

This was probably the first transaction, in the American Colonies, relating to the freedom of the press; and it is not less remarkable for the assumption of power on the part of the legislature, than for their disregard of the first principles and established forms of law.

No change took place in the character of the paper, and six months afterwards, January, 1723, he was again arraigned upon a similar charge. The resentment of the ruling powers, stimulated by the clergy, had been gaining heat during the whole time, and now pushed them to more arbitrary measures. They condescended, however, to specify a particular article, as affording the ground of their proceedings. This was an essay on *Hypocrisy*, in which hypocrites of various descriptions were roughly handled, but no individual or class of men was mentioned. The most objectionable paragraphs in this essay are the following :—

"Religion is indeed the principal thing, but too much of it is worse than none at all. The world abounds with knaves and villains; but, of all knaves, the religious knave is the worst, and villanies acted under the cloak of religion the most execrable. Moral honesty, though it will not itself carry a man to heaven, yet I am sure there is no going thither without it."

"But are there such men as these in thee, O New England? Heaven forbid there should be any: but, alas! it is to be feared the number is

c 2

At length, a fresh difference arising between my brother and me, I took upon me to assert my freedom; presuming that he would not venture to produce the new indentures. It was not fair in me to take this advantage, and this I therefore reckon one of the first *errata* of my life; but the unfairness of it weighed little with me when under the impressions of resentment for the blows his passion too often urged him to bestow upon me. Though he was otherwise not an ill-natured man; perhaps I was too saucy and provoking.

When he found I would leave him, he took care to prevent my getting employment in any other printing-house of the town, by going round and speaking to every master, who accordingly refused to give me work. I then thought of going to New York, as the nearest place where there was a printer. And I was rather inclined to leave Boston, when I reflected, that I had already made myself a little obnoxious to the governing party, and, from the arbitrary proceedings of the Assembly in my brother's case, it was likely I might, if I stayed, soon bring myself into scrapes; and further, that my indiscreet disputations about religion began to make me pointed at with horror by good people, as an infidel and atheist. I concluded, therefore, to remove to New York; but my father now siding with my brother, I was sensible, that, if I attempted to go openly, means would be used to prevent me. My friend Collins, therefore, undertook to manage my flight. He agreed with the captain of a New York sloop to take me, under pretence of my being a young man of his acquaintance, that had an intrigue with a girl of bad character, whose parents would compel me to marry her, and that I could neither appear nor come away publicly. I sold my books to raise a little money, was taken on board the sloop privately, had a fair wind, and in three days found myself at New York, near three hundred miles from my home, at the age of seventeen (October, 1723), without the least recommendation, or knowledge of any person in the place, and very little money in my pocket.

not small. '*Give me an honest man,*' say some, '*for all a religious man ;*' a distinction which, I confess, I never heard of before. The whole country suffers for the villanies of a few such wolves in sheep's clothing, and we are all represented as a pack of knaves and hypocrites for their sakes."—ED.

CHAPTER II.

THE inclination I had had for the sea was by this time done away, or I might now have gratified it. But having another profession, and conceiving myself a pretty good workman, I offered my services to a printer of the place, old Mr. William Bradford, who had been the first printer in Pennsylvania, but had removed thence, in consequence of a quarrel with the governor, George Keith. He could give me no employment having little to do, and hands enough already; but he said. "My son at Philadelphia has lately lost his principal hand, Aquila Rose, by death; if you go thither, I believe he may employ you." Philadelphia was one hundred miles further; I set out however in a boat for Amboy, leaving my chest and things to follow me round by sea.

In crossing the bay, we met with a squall that tore our rotten sails to pieces, prevented our getting into the Kill, and drove us upon Long Island. In our way, a drunken Dutchman, who was a passenger too, fell overboard; when he was sinking, I reached through the water to his shock pate, and drew him up, so that we got him in again. His ducking sobered him a little, and he went to sleep, taking first out of his pocket a book, which he desired I would dry for him. It proved to be my old favourite author, Bunyan's *Pilgrim's Progress*, in Dutch, finely printed on good paper, copper cuts, a dress better than I had ever seen it wear in its own language. I have since found that it has been translated into most of the languages of Europe, and suppose it has been more generally read than any other book, except perhaps the Bible. . Honest John was the first that I know of, who mixed narration and dialogue; a method of writing very engaging to the reader, who in the most interesting parts finds himself, as it were, admitted into the company and present at the conversation. Defoe has imitated him successfully in his *Robinson Crusoe*, in his *Moll Flanders*, and other pieces; and Richardson has done the same in his *Pamela*, &c.

On approaching the island, we found it was in a place where there could be no landing, there being a great surge on the stony beach. So we dropped anchor, and swung out our cable towards the shore. Some people came down to the shore, and hallooed to us, as we did to them; but the wind was so high, and the surge so loud, that we could not understand each other. There were some small boats near the shore, and we made signs, and called to them to fetch us; but they either did not comprehend us, or it was impracticable, so they went off. Night approaching, we had no remedy but to have patience till the wind abated; and in the mean time the boatmen and myself concluded to sleep, if we could; and so we crowded into the hatches where we joined the Dutchman, who was still wet, and the spray, breaking over the head of our boat, leaked through to us, so that we were soon almost as wet as he. In this manner we lay all night, with very little rest; but, the wind abating the next day, we made a shift to reach Amboy before night; having been thirty hours on the water, without victuals, or any drink but a bottle of filthy rum; the water we sailed on being salt.

In the evening I found myself very feverish, and went to bed; but, having read somewhere that cold water drunk plentifully was good for a fever, I followed the prescription, and swet plentifully most of the night. My fever left me, and in the morning, crossing the ferry, I proceeded on my journey on foot, having fifty miles to go to Burlington, where I was told I should find boats, that would carry me the rest of the way to Philadelphia.

It rained very hard all the day; I was thoroughly soaked, and by noon a good deal tired; so I stopped at a poor inn, where I stayed all night; beginning now to wish I had never left home. I made so miserable a figure, too, that I found, by the questions asked me, I was suspected to be some runaway indentured servant, and in danger of being taken up on that suspicion. However, I proceeded next day, and got in the evening to an inn, within eight or ten miles of Burlington, kept by one Dr. Brown. He entered into conversation with me while I took some refreshment, and, finding I had read a little, became very obliging and friendly. Our acquaintance continued all the rest of his life. He had been, I imagine, an ambulatory quack doctor, for there was no town in England, nor any country in Europe, of which he could not give a very particular account. He had some letters, and was ingenious, but he was an infidel, and wickedly undertook, some years after, to turn the Bible into doggrel verse; as Cotton had formerly done with Virgil. By this means he set many facts in a ridiculous light, and might have done mischief with weak minds, if his work had been published; but it never was.

At his house I lay that night, and arrived the next morning at Burlington; but had the mortification to find, that the regular boats were gone a little before, and no other expected to go before Tuesday, this being Saturday. Wherefore I returned to an old woman in the town, of whom I had bought some gingerbread to eat on the water, and asked her advice. She proposed to lodge me, till a passage by some other boat occurred. I accepted her offer, being much fatigued by travelling on foot. Understanding I was a printer, she would have had me remain in that town and follow my business; being ignorant what stock was necessary to begin with. She was very hospitable, gave me a dinner of ox-cheek with great good will, accepting only of a pot of ale in return; and I thought myself fixed till Tuesday should come. However, walking in the evening by the side of the river, a boat came by, which I found was going towards Philadelphia with several people in her. They took me in, and, as there was no wind, we rowed all the way; and about midnight, not having yet seen the city, some of the company were confident we must have passed it, and would row no further; the others knew not where we were, so we put towards the shore, got into a creek, landed near an old fence, with the rails of which we made a fire, the night being cold, in October, and there we remained till daylight. Then one of the company knew the place to be Cooper's Creek, a little above Philadelphia, which we saw as soon as we got out of the creek, and arrived there about eight or nine o'clock on the Sunday morning, and landed at Market-street wharf.

I have been the more particular in this description of my journey, and shall be so of my first entry into that city, that you may in your mind compare such unlikely beginnings with the figure I have since made there. I was in my working dress, my best clothes coming round by sea. I was dirty from my being so long in the boat. My pockets were stuffed out with shirts and stockings, and I knew no one, nor where to look for lodging. Fatigued with walking, rowing, and the want of sleep, I was very hungry; and my whole stock of cash consisted in a single dollar, and about a shilling in copper coin, which I gave to the boatmen for my passage. At first they refused it, on account of my having rowed; but I insisted on their taking it. Man is sometimes more generous when he has little money than when he has plenty; perhaps to prevent his being thought to have but little.

I walked towards the top of the street, gazing about till near Market Street, where I met a boy with bread. I had often made a meal of dry bread, and, inquiring where he had bought it, I went immediately to the baker's he directed me to. I asked for biscuits, meaning such as we had at Boston; that sort, it seems, was not made in Philadelphia. I then asked for a threepenny loaf, and was told they had none. Not knowing the different prices, nor the names of the different sorts of bread, I told him to give me threepenny worth of any sort. He gave me accordingly three great puffy rolls. I was surprised at the quantity, but took it, and, having no room in my pockets, walked off with a roll under each arm, and eating the other. Thus I went up Market Street as far as Fourth Street, passing by the door of Mr. Read, my future wife's father; when she, standing at the door, saw me, and thought I made, as I certainly did, a most awkward, ridiculous appearance. Then I turned, and went down Chestnut Street and part of Walnut Street, eating my roll all the way; and, coming round, found myself again at Market-Street wharf, near the boat I came in, to which I went for a draught of the river water; and, being filled with one of my rolls, gave the other two to a woman and her child that came down the river in the boat with us, and were waiting to go farther.

Thus refreshed, I walked again up the street, which, by this time, had many clean-dressed people in it, who were all walking the same way. I joined them, and thereby was led into the great meeting-house of the Quakers, near the market. I sat down among them, and, after looking round a while, and hearing nothing said, being very drowsy through labour and want of rest the preceding night, I fell fast asleep, and continued so till the meeting broke up, when some one was kind enough to rouse me. This, therefore, was the first house I was in, or slept in, in Philadelphia.

I then walked down towards the river, and, looking in the faces of every one, I met a young Quaker man, whose countenance pleased me; and, accosting him, requested he would tell me where a stranger could get a lodging. We were then near the sign of the Three Mariners. "Here," said he, "is a house where they receive strangers; but it is not a reputable one: if thee wilt walk with me, I'll show thee a better one;" and he conducted me to the Crooked Billet, in Water Street. There I got a dinner; and while I was eating, several questions were asked me, as, from my youth and appearance, I was suspected of being a runaway.

After dinner, my host having shown me to a bed, I laid myself on it without undressing, and slept till six in the evening, when I was called to supper. I went to bed again very early, and slept very soundly till next morning. Then I dressed myself as neat as I could, and went to Andrew Bradford, the printer's. I found in the shop the old man his father, whom I had seen at New York, and who, travelling on horseback, had got to Philadelphia before me. He introduced me to his son, who received me civilly, gave me a breakfast, but told me he did not at present want a hand, being lately supplied with one; but there was another printer in town, lately set up, one Keimer, who perhaps might employ me; if not, I should be welcome to lodge at his house, and he would give me a little work to do now and then, till fuller business should offer.

The old gentleman said he would go with me to the new printer; and when we found him, "Neighbour," said Bradford, "I have brought to see you a young man of your business: perhaps you may want such a one." He asked me a few questions, put a composing stick in my hand to see how I worked, and then said he would employ me soon, though he had just then nothing for me to do. And taking old Bradford, whom he had never seen before, to be one of the town's-people that had a good will for him, entered into a conversation on his present undertaking and prospects; while Bradford, not discovering that he was the other printer's father, on Keimer's saying he expected soon to get the greatest part of the business into his own hands, drew him on, by artful questions, and starting little doubts, to explain all his views, what influence he relied on, and in what manner he intended to proceed. I, who stood by and heard all, saw immediately that one was a crafty old sophister, and the other a true novice. Bradford left me with Keimer, who was greatly surprised when I told him who the old man was.

The printing-house, I found, consisted of an old, damaged press, and a small, worn-out fount of English types, which he was using himself, composing an *Elegy* on Aquila Rose, before mentioned; an ingenious young man, of excellent character, much respected in the town, secretary to the Assembly, and a pretty poet. Keimer made verses too, but very indifferently. He could not be said to *write* them, for his method was to compose them in the types directly out of his head. There being no copy, but one pair of cases, and the *Elegy* probably

requiring all the letter, no one could help him. I endeavoured
to put his press (which he had not yet used, and of which he
understood nothing) into order to be worked with; and, promising to come and print off his *Elegy*, as soon as he should
have got it ready, I returned to Bradford's, who gave me a
little job to do for the present, and there I lodged and dieted.
A few days after, Keimer sent for me to print off the *Elegy*.
And now he had got another pair of cases, and a pamphlet to
reprint, on which he set me to work.

These two printers I found poorly qualified for their business. Bradford had not been bred to it, and was very illiterate;
and Keimer, though something of a scholar, was a mere compositor, knowing nothing of presswork. He had been one of
the French prophets, and could act their enthusiastic agitations.
At this time he did not profess any particular religion, but
something of all on occasion; was very ignorant of the world,
and had, as I afterwards found, a good deal of the knave in
his composition. He did not like my lodging at Bradford's
while I worked with him. He had a house, indeed, but without furniture, so he could not lodge me; but he got me a
lodging at Mr. Read's, before mentioned, who was the owner
of his house; and, my chest of clothes being come by this
time, I made rather a more respectable appearance in the eyes
of Miss Read than I had done when she first happened to see
me eating my roll in the street.

I began now to have some acquaintance among the young
people of the town that were lovers of reading, with whom I
spent my evenings very pleasantly; and gained money by my
industry and frugality. I lived very contented, and forgot
Boston as much, as I could, and did not wish should to be known
where I resided except to my friend Collins, who was in the
secret, and kept it faithfully. At length, however, an incident
happened that occasioned my return home much sooner than
I had intended. I had a brother-in-law, Robert Holmes,
master of a sloop that traded between Boston and Delaware.
He being at Newcastle, forty miles below Philadelphia, and
hearing of me, wrote me a letter mentioning the grief of my
relations and friends in Boston at my abrupt departure,
assuring me of their good-will to me, and that everything
would be accommodated to my mind if I would return; to
which he entreated me earnestly. I wrote an answer to his
letter, thanked him for his advice, but stated my reasons for
quitting Boston so fully and in such a light as to convince

him that I was not so much in the wrong as he had appre-
nended.

Sir William Keith, Governor of the province, was then at
Newcastle, and Captain Holmes, happening to be in company
with him when my letter came to hand, spoke to him of me,
and showed him the letter. The governor read it, and
seemed surprised when he was told my age. He said I
appeared a young man of promising parts, and therefore
should be encouraged; the printers at Philadelphia were
wretched ones; and, if I would set up there, he made no
doubt I should succeed; for his part he would procure me the
public business, and do me every other service in his power.
This my brother-in-law Holmes afterwards told me in Boston;
but I knew as yet nothing of it; when one day, Keimer and
I. being at work together near the window, we saw the
Governor and another gentleman (who proved to be Colonel
French, of Newcastle, in the province of Delaware,) finely
dressed, come directly across the street to our house, and
heard them at the door.

Keimer ran down immediately, thinking it a visit to him;
but the Governor inquired for me, came up, and with a con-
descension and politeness I had been quite unused to, made
him many compliments, desired to be acquainted with me,
blamed me kindly for not having made myself known to him,
when I first came to the place, and would have me away with
him to the tavern, where he was going with Colonel French to
taste, as he said, some excellent madeira. I was not a little
surprised, and Keimer stared with astonishment. I went
however with the Governor and Colonel French to a tavern,
at the corner of Third Street, and over the madeira he proposed my setting up my business. He stated the probabilities
of my success, and both he and Colonel French assured me
I should have their interest and influence to obtain for me the
public business of both governments. And as I expressed
doubts that my father would assist me in it, Sir William said
he would give me a letter to him, in which he would set forth
the advantages, and he did not doubt he should determine
him to comply. So it was concluded I should return to
Boston by the first vessel, with the Governor's letter to my
father. In the meantime it was to be kept a secret, and I
went on working with Keimer as usual. The Governor sent
for me now and then to dine with him, which I considered a
great honour; more particularly as he conversed with me in
a most affable, familiar, and friendly manner.

About the end of April, 1724, a little vessel offered for
Boston. I took leave of Keimer, as going to see my friends.
The Governor gave me an ample letter, saying many flattering
things of me to my father, and strongly recommending the
project of my setting up at Philadelphia, as a thing that would
make my fortune. We struck on a shoal in going down the
bay, and sprung a leak; we had a blustering time at sea, and
were obliged to pump almost continually, at which I took
my turn. We arrived safe however at Boston in about a
fortnight. I had been absent seven months, and my
friends had heard nothing of me; for my brother Homes was
not yet returned, and had not written about me. My unexpected appearance surprised the family; all were however
very glad to see me, and made me welcome, except my
brother. I went to see him at his printing-house. I was
better dressed than ever while in his service, having a genteel
new suit from head to foot, a watch, and my pockets lined
with near five pounds sterling in silver. He received me not
very frankly, looked me all over, and turned to his work again.

The journeymen were inquisitive where I had been, what
sort of a country it was, and how I liked it. I praised it
much, and the happy life I led in it, expressing strongly my
intention of returning to it; and, one of them asking what
kind of money we had there, I produced a handful of silver,
and spread it before them, which was a kind of *raree-show*
they had not been used to, paper being the money of Boston.
Then I took an opportunity of letting them see my watch;
and lastly (my brother still grum and sullen) gave them a
dollar to drink, and took my leave. This visit of mine offended him extremely. For, when my mother sometime
after spoke to him of a reconciliation, and of her wish to see
us on good terms together, and that we might live for the
future as brothers, he said, I had insulted him in such a
manner before his people that he could never forget or
forgive it. In this, however, he was mistaken.

My father received the Governor's letter with some surprise; but said little of it to me for some time. Captain
Holmes returning, he showed it to him, and asked him, if he
knew Sir William Keith, and what kind of a man he was;
adding that he must be of small discretion to think of setting
a youth up in business who wanted three years to arrive at
man's estate. Holmes said what he could in favour of the
project, but my father was decidedly against it, and at last
gave a flat denial. He wrote a civil letter to Sir William

thanking him for the patronage he had so kindly offered me,
and declined to assist me as yet in setting up, I being in his
opinion too young to be trusted with the management of an
undertaking so important, and for which the preparation
required a considerable expenditure.

My *old* companion Collins, who was a clerk in the post-
office, pleased with the account I gave him of my new
country, determined to go thither also; and, while I waited
for my father's determination, he set out before me by land to
Rhode Island, leaving his books, which were a pretty collection in mathematics and natural philosophy, to come with
mine and me to New York; where he proposed to wait for me.

My father, though he did not approve Sir William's proposition, was yet pleased that I had been able to obtain so
advantageous a character from a person of such note where I
had resided; and that I had been so industrious and careful
as to equip myself so handsomely in so short a time; therefore seeing no prospect of an accommodation between my
brother and me, he gave his consent to my returning again to
Philadelphia, advised me to behave respectfully to the people
there, endeavour to obtain the general esteem, and avoid
lampooning and libelling, to which he thought I had too much
inclination; telling me, that by steady industry and prudent
parsimony, I might save enough by the time I was one-and-
twenty to set me up; and that if I came near the matter he
would help me out with the rest. This was all I could obtain,
except some small gifts as tokens of his and my mother's
love, when I embarked again for New York; now with their
approbation and their blessing.

The sloop putting in at Newport, Rhode Island, I visited
my brother John, who had been married and settled there
some years. He received me very affectionately, for he
always loved me. A friend of his, one Vernon, having some
money due to him in Pennsylvania, about thirty-five pounds
currency, desired I would recover it for him, and keep it
till I had his directions what to employ it in. Accordingly
he gave me an order to receive it. This business afterwards
occasioned me a good deal of uneasiness.

At Newport we took in a number of passengers, amongst
whom were two young women travelling together, and a sensible, matron-like Quaker lady, with her servants. I had
shown an obliging disposition to render her some little services, which probably impressed her with sentiments of good

will towards me; for, when she witnessed the daily growing familiarity between the young women and myself, which they appeared to encourage, she took me aside and said, "Young man, I am concerned for thee, as thou hast no friend with thee, and seems not to know much of the world, or of the snares youth is exposed to; depend upon it, these are very bad women; I can see it by all their actions; and if thee art not upon thy guard, they will draw thee into some danger; they are strangers to thee, and I advise thee, in a friendly concern for thy welfare, to have no acquaintance with them." As I seemed at first not so think so ill of them as she did, she mentioned some things she had observed and heard, that had escaped my notice, but now convinced me she was right. I thanked her for her kind advice, and promised to follow it. When we arrived at New York they told me where they lived, and invited me to come and see them, but I avoided it, and it was well I did; for the next day the captain missed a silver spoon and some other things, that had been taken out of his cabin, and, knowing that these were a couple of strumpets, he got a warrant to search their lodgings, found the stolen goods, and had the thieves punished. So though we had escaped a sunken rock, which we scraped upon in the passage, I thought this escape of rather more importance to me.

At New York I found my friend Collins, who had arrived there some time before me. We had been intimate from children, and had read the same books together; but he had the advantage of more time for reading and studying, and a wonderful genius for mathematical learning, in which he far outstripped me. While I lived in Boston, most of my hours of leisure for conversation were spent with him, and he continued a sober as well as industrious lad; was much respected for his learning by several of the clergy and other gentlemen, and seemed to promise making a good figure in life. But, during my absence he had acquired a habit of drinking brandy, and I found by his own account, as well as that of others, that he had been drunk every day since his arrival at New York, and behaved himself in a very extravagant manner. He had gamed too and lost his money, so that I was obliged to discharge his lodgings, and defray his expenses on the road and at Philadelphia, which proved a great burden to me.

The then Governor of New York, Burnet, (son of Bishop Burnet,) hearing from the captain that one of the passengers had a great many books on board, desired him to bring me to see him. I waited on him, and should have taken Collins with me had he been sober. The Governor received me with great civility, showed me his library, which was a considerable one, and we had a good deal of conversation relative to books and authors. This was the second Governor who had done me the honour to take notice of me, and, for a poor boy like me, it was very pleasing.

We proceeded to Philadelphia. I received in the way Vernon's money, without which we could hardly have finished our journey. Collins wished to be employed in some counting-house; but, whether they discovered his dram-drinking by his breath or by his behaviour, though he had some recommendations, he met with no success in any application, and continued lodging and boarding at the same house with me, and at my expense. Knowing I had that money of Vernon's, he was continually borrowing of me, still promising repayment as soon as he should be in business. At length he had got so much of it, that I was distressed to think what I should do in case of being called on to remit it.

His drinking continued, about which we sometimes quarrelled, for when a little intoxicated he was very irritable. Once in a boat on the Delaware with some other young men, he refused to row in his turn. "I will be rowed home," said he. "We will not row you," said I. "You must," said he, "or stay all night on the water, just as you please." The others said, "Let us row, what signifies it!" But, my mind being soured with his other conduct, I continued to refuse. So he swore he would make me row, or throw me overboard; and coming along stepping on the thwarts towards me, when he came up and struck at me, I clapped my head under his thighs, and, rising, pitched him headforemost into the river. I knew he was a good swimmer, and so was under little concern about him; but before he could get round to lay hold of the boat, we had with a few strokes pulled her out of his reach; and whenever he drew near the boat, we asked him if he would row, striking a few strokes to slide her away from him. He was ready to stifle with vexation, and obstinately would not promise to row. Finding him at last beginning to tire we drew him into the boat, and brought him home dripping wet. We hardly exchanged a civil word after this adventure. At length a West India captain, who had a commission to procure a preceptor for the sons of a gentleman at Barbadoes, met with him, and proposed to carry him thither to fill that situation. He accepted, and promised to remit me what he owed me out of the first money he should receive, but I never heard of him after.

The violation of my trust respecting Vernon's money was one of the first great *errata* of my life; and this showed that my father was not much out in his judgment, when he considered me as too young to manage business. But Sir William, on reading his letter, said he was too prudent, that there was a great difference in persons; and discretion did not always accompany years, nor was youth always without it. " But since he will not set you up, I will do it myself. Give me an inventory of the things necessary to be had from England, and I will send for them. You shall repay me when you are able; I am resolved to have a good printer here, and I am sure you must succeed." This was spoken with such an appearance of cordiality, that I had not the least doubt of his meaning what he said. I had hitherto kept the proposition of my setting up a secret in Philadelphia, and I still kept it. Had it been known that I depended on the Governor, probably some friend, that knew him better, would have advised me not to rely on him, as I afterwards heard it as his known character to be liberal of promises, which he never meant to keep. Yet, unsolicited as he was by me, how could I think his generous offers insincere? I believed him one of the best men in the world.

I presented him an inventory of a little printing-house, amounting, by my computation, to about one hundred pounds sterling. He liked it, but asked me, if my being on the spot in England to choose the types, and see that every thing was good of the kind, might not be of some advantage. " Then," said he, " when there, you may make acquaintance, and establishing correspondences in the bookselling and stationery line." I agreed that this might be advantageous. "Then," said he, "get yourself ready to go with *Annis*," which was the annual ship, and the only one, at that time, usually passing between London and Philadelphia. But as it would be some months before *Annis* sailed, I continued working with Keimer, fretting extremely about the money Collins had got from me, and in great apprehensions of being called upon for it by Vernon; this, however, did not happen for some years after.

I believe I have omitted mentioning, that in my first voyage from Boston to Philadelphia, being becalmed off

Block Island, our crew employed themselves in catching cod and hauled up a great number. Till then, I had stuck to my resolution to eat nothing that had had life; and on this occasion I considered, according to my master Tryon, the taking every fish as a kind of unprovoked murder, since none of them had, or could do us any injury, that might justify this massacre. All this seemed very reasonable. But I had been formerly a great lover of fish, and when it came out of the frying-pan it smelt admirably well. I balanced some time between principle and inclination, till, recollecting that when the fish were opened I saw smaller fish taken out of their stomachs, then, thought I, " If you eat one another, I don't see why we may not eat you;" so I dined upon cod very heartily, and have since continued to eat as other people, returning only now and then occasionally to a vegetable diet. So convenient a thing it is to be a *reasonable creature*, since it enables one to find or make a *reason* for every thing one has a mind to do.

Keimer and I lived on a pretty good familiar footing, and agreed tolerably well, for he suspected nothing of my setting up. He retained a great deal of his old enthusiasm, and loved argumentation; we therefore had many disputations. I used to work him so with my Socratic method, and had trepanned him so often by questions apparently so distant from any point we had in hand, yet by degrees leading to the point, and bringing him into difficulties and contradictions, that at last he grew ridiculously cautious, and would hardly answer me the most common question, without asking first, " What do you intend to infer from that?" However, it gave him so high an opinion of my abilities in the confuting way, that he seriously proposed my being his colleague in a project he had of setting up a new sect. He was to preach the doctrines, and I was to confound all opponents. When he came to explain with me upon the doctrines, I found several conundrums, which I objected to, unless I might have my way a little too, and introduce some of mine.

Keimer wore his beard at full length, because somewhere in the Mosaic law it is said, " *Thou shalt not mar the corners of thy beard.*" He likewise kept the seventh day, Sabbath; and these two points were essential with him. I disliked both, but agreed to them on condition of his adopting the doctrine of not using animal food. " I doubt," said he, " my constitution will not bear it." I assured him it would, and that he would be the better for it. He was usually a great eater, and I wished to give myself some diversion in half starving him. He consented to try the practice, if I would keep him company. I did so, and we held it for three months. Our provisions were purchased, cooked, and brought to us regularly by a woman in the neighbourhood, who had from me a list of forty dishes, which she prepared for us at different times, in which there entered neither fish, flesh, nor fowl. This whim suited me the better at this time from the cheapness of it, not costing us above eighteen pence sterling each per week. I have since kept several lents most strictly, leaving the common diet for that, and that for the common, abruptly, without the least inconvenience; so that I think there is little in the advice of making those changes by easy gradations. I went on pleasantly, but poor Keimer suffered grievously, grew tired of the project, longed for the fleshpots of Egypt, and ordered a roast pig. He invited me and two women friends to dine with him; but, it being brought too soon upon table, he could not resist the temptation, and ate the whole before we came.

I had made some courtship during this time to Miss Read. I had a great respect and affection for her, and had some reasons to believe she had the same for me; but, as I was about to take a long voyage, and we were both very young, only a little above eighteen, it was thought most prudent by her mother to prevent our going too far at present; as a marriage, if it was to take place, would be more convenient after my return, when I should be, as I hoped, set up in my business. Perhaps, too, she thought my expectations not so well founded as I imagined them to be.

My chief acquaintances at this time were Charles Osborne, Joseph Watson, and James Ralph; all lovers of reading. The two first were clerks to an eminent scrivener or conveyancer in the town, Charles Brockden, the other was a clerk to a merchant. Watson was a pious, sensible young man, of great integrity; the others rather more lax in their principles of religion, particularly Ralph, who, as well as Collins, had been unsettled by me; for which they both made me suffer. Osborne was sensible, candid, frank; sincere and affectionate to his friends; but, in literary matters, too fond of criticism. Ralph was ingenious, genteel in his manners, and extremely eloquent; I think I never knew a prettier talker. Both were great admirers of poetry, and began to try their hands in little pieces. Many pleasant walks we have had together on Sundays in the woods, on the banks of the Schuylkill, where we read to one another, and conferred on what we had read.

Ralph was inclined to give himself up entirely to poetry, not doubting that he might make great proficiency in it, and even make his fortune by it. He pretended that the greatest poets must, when they first began to write, have committed as many faults as he did. Osborne endeavoured to dissuade him, assured him he had no genius for poetry, and advised him to think of nothing beyond the business he was bred to; that in the mercantile way, though he had no stock, he might by his diligence and punctuality recommend himself to employment as a factor, and in time acquire wherewith to trade on his own account. I approved for my part the amusing one's self with poetry now and then, so far as to improve's one language, but no farther.

On this it was proposed that we should each of us, at our next meeting, produce a piece of our own composing, in order to improve by our mutual observations, criticisms, and corrections. As language and expression were what we had in view, we excluded all considerations of invention, by agreeing that the task should be a version of the eighteenth Psalm, which describes the descent of a Deity. When the time of our meeting drew nigh, Ralph called on me first, and let me know his piece was ready. I told him I had been busy, and having little inclination, had done nothing. He then showed me his piece for my opinion, and I much approved it, as it appeared to me to have great merit. "Now," said he, "Osborne never will allow the least merit in anything of mine, but makes a thousand criticisms out of mere envy. He is not so jealous of you; I wish, therefore, you would take this piece and produce it as yours. I will pretend not to have had time, and so produce nothing. We shall then hear what he will say to it." It was agreed, and I immediately transcribed it, that it might appear in my own hand.

We met. Watson's performance was read; there were some beauties in it, but many defects. Osborne's was read; it was much better. Ralph did it justice; remarked some faults, but applauded the beauties. He himself had nothing to produce. I was backward, seemed desirous of being excused, had not had sufficient time to correct, &c. But no excuse could be admitted; produce I must. It was read and repeated. Watson and Osborne gave up the contest, and joined in applauding it. Ralph only made some criticisms, and proposed some amendments; but I defended my text. Osborne was severe against Ralph, and told me he was no better able to criticize than compose verses. As these two were returning home, Osborne expressed himself still more strongly in favour of what he thought my production; having before refrained, as he said, lest I should think he meant to flatter me. "But who would have imagined," said he, "that Franklin was capable of such a performance; such painting, such force, such fire! He has even improved on the original. In common conversation he seems to have no choice of words; he hesitates and blunders, and yet, good God, how he writes!" When we next met, Ralph discovered the trick we had played, and Osborne was laughed at.

This transaction fixed Ralph in his resolution of becoming a poet. I did all I could to dissuade him from it, but he continued scribbling verses till Pope cured him. He became, however, a pretty good prose writer. More of him here-after.* But, as I may not have occasion to mention the other two, I shall just remark here, that Watson died in my arms a few years after, much lamented, being the best of our set. Osborne went to the West Indies, where he became an eminent lawyer and made money, but died young. He and I had made a serious agreement, that the one who happened first to die should, if possible, make a friendly visit to the other, and acquaint him how he found things in that separate state. But he never fulfilled his promise.

The Governor, seeming to like my company, had me fre-quently at his house; and his setting me up was always mentioned as a fixed thing. I was to take with me letters

---

* Ralph obtained much celebrity as a political and historical writer. He also wrote poetry and plays, but with less success. He published "Night," a poem; and another poem, called "Sawney." In this latter he abused Swift, Pope, and Gay. In revenge, Pope introduced his name into the "Dunciad."

> "Silence, ye wolves, while Ralph to Cynthia howls,
>   And makes *Night* hideous; answer him, ye owls."

He wrote a much approved work, entitled "Use and Abuse of Par-liaments;" and also a "History of England during the reign of William the Third," in two folio volumes. Alluding to this work, Fox pro-nounces the author "a historian of great acuteness, as well as diligence, but who falls sometimes into the common error of judging by the event." Ralph produced also many political pamphlets, and was em-ployed by the ministry at different times to promote their aims with his pen. For these services he was pensioned.—ED.

recommendatory to a number of his friends, besides the letter of credit to furnish me with the necessary money for pur- chasing the press, types, paper, &c. For these letters I was appointed to call at different times, when they were to be ready ; but a future time was still named. Thus we went on till the ship—whose departure, too, had been several times postponed—was on the point of sailing. Then, when I called to take my leave and receive the letters, his secretary, Dr. Baird, came out to me and said the Governor was extremely busy in writing, but would be down at Newcastle before the ship, and then the letters would be delivered to me.

Ralph, though married, and having one child, had deter- mined to accompany me in this voyage. It was thought he intended to establish a correspondence, and obtain goods to sell on commission ; but I found after, that having some cause of discontent with his wife's relations, he proposed to leave her on their hands, and never to return to America. Having taken leave of my friends, and exchanged promises with Miss Read, I quitted Philadelphia in the ship, which anchored at Newcastle. The Governor was there ; but when I went to his lodging, his secretary came to me from him with expres- sions of the greatest regret that he could not then see me, being engaged in business of the utmost importance ; but that he would send the letters to me on board, wishing me heartily a good voyage and a speedy return, &c. I returned on board a little puzzled, but still not doubting.

CHAPTER III.

MR. ANDREW HAMILTON, a celebrated lawyer of Phila- delphia, had taken his passage in the same ship for himself and son, with Mr. Denham, a Quaker merchant, and Messrs. Oniam and Russel, masters of an iron work in Maryland, who had engaged the great cabin ; so that Ralph and I were forced to take up with a berth in the steerage, and none on board knowing us, were considered as ordinary persons. But Mr. Hamilton and his son (it was James, since Governor,) returned from Newcastle to Philadelphia ; the father being recalled by a great fee to plead for a seized ship. And, just before we sailed, Colonel French coming on board, and showing me great respect, I was more taken notice of, and, with my friend Ralph, invited by the other gentlemen to come into the cabin, there being now room. Accordingly we removed thither.

Understanding that Colonel French had brought on board the Governor's despatches, I asked the captain for those letters that were to be under my care. He said all were put into the bag together; and he could not then come at them; but, before we landed in England, I should have an opportunity of picking them out; so I was satisfied for the present, and we proceeded on our voyage. We had a sociable company in the cabin, and lived uncommonly well, having the addition of all Mr. Hamilton's stores, who had laid in plentifully. In this passage Mr. Denham contracted a friendship for me, that continued during his life. The voyage was otherwise not a pleasant one, as we had a great deal of bad weather.

When we came into the Channel, the captain kept his word with me, and gave me an opportunity of examining the bag for the Governor's letters. I found some upon which my name was put as under my care. I picked out six or seven, that, by the handwriting, I thought might be the promised letters, especially as one of them was addressed to Baskett, the King's printer, and another to some stationer. We arrived in London the 24th December, 1724. I waited upon the stationer, who came first in my way, delivering the letter as from Governor Keith. "I don't know such a person," said he; but, opening the letter, "oh! this is from Riddlesden. I have lately found him to be a complete rascal, and I will have nothing to do with him, nor receive any letters from him." So putting the letter into my hand, he turned on his heel and left me to serve some customer. I was surprised to find these were not the Governor's letters; and, after recollecting and comparing circumstances, I began to doubt his sincerity. I found my friend Denham, and opened the whole affair to him. He let me into Keith's character, told me there was not the least probability that he had written any letters for me; that no one, who knew him, had the smallest dependence on him; and he laughed at the idea of the Governor's giving me a letter of credit, having, as he said, no credit to give. On my expressing some concern about what I should do, he advised me to endeavour getting some employment in the way of my business. "Among the printers here," said he, "you will improve yourself, and when you return to America, you will set up to greater advantage."

We both of us happened to know, as well as the stationer, that Riddlesden, the attorney, was a very knave. He had half ruined Miss Read's father, by persuading him to be bound for him. By his letter it appeared there was a secret scheme on foot to the prejudice of Mr. Hamilton (supposed to be then coming over with us); that Keith was concerned in it with Riddlesden. Denham, who was a friend of Hamilton's, thought he ought to be acquainted with it; so, when he arrived in England, which was soon after, partly from resentment and ill will to Keith and Riddlesden, and partly from good will to him, I waited on him, and gave him the letter. He thanked me cordially, the information being of importance to him; and from that time he became my friend, greatly to my advantage afterwards on many occasions.

But what shall we think of a Governor playing such pitiful tricks, and imposing so grossly on a poor ignorant boy! It was a habit he had acquired. He wished to please everybody; and, having little to give, he gave expectations. He was otherwise an ingenious, sensible man, a pretty good writer, and a good Governor for the people; though not for his constituents, the Proprietaries, whose instructions he sometimes disregarded. Several of our best laws were of his planning, and passed during his administration.

Ralph and I were inseparable companions. We took lodgings together in Little Britain at three shillings and sixpence a week; as much as we could then afford. He found some relations, but they were poor, and unable to assist him. He now let me know his intentions of remaining in London, and that he never meant to return to Philadelphia. He had brought no money with him; the whole he could muster having been expended in paying his passage. I had fifteen pistoles; so he borrowed occasionally of me to subsist, while he was looking out for business. He first endeavoured to get into the playhouse, believing himself qualified for an actor; but Wilkes,* to whom he applied, advised him candidly not to think of that employment, as it was impossible he should succeed in it. Then he proposed to Roberts, a publisher in Pater Noster Row, to write for him a weekly paper like the *Spectator*, on certain conditions; which Roberts did not approve. Then he endeavoured to get employment as a hackney writer, to copy for the stationers and lawyers about the Temple; but could not find a vacancy.

For myself, I immediately got into work at Palmer's, a

* A comedian of eminence.

famous printing-house in Bartholomew Close, where I continued near a year.   I was pretty diligent, but I spent with
Ralph a good deal of my earnings at plays and public amusements.   We had nearly consumed all my pistoles, and now
just rubbed on from hand to mouth.   He seemed quite to
have forgotten his wife and child; and I by degrees my en-
gagements with Miss Read, to whom I never wrote more than
one letter, and that was to let her know I was not likely soon
to return.   This was another of the great *errata* of my life,
which I could wish to correct, if I were to live it over again.
In fact, by our expenses, I was constantly kept unable to pay
my passage.

At Palmer's I was employed in composing for the second
edition of Wollaston's *Religion of Nature*.   Some of his
reasonings not appearing to me well founded, I wrote a little
metaphysical piece in which I made remarks on them.   It
was entitled, *A Dissertation on Liberty and Necessity, Pleasure and Pain*.   I inscribed it to my friend Ralph; I printed
a small number.   It occasioned my being more considered by
Mr. Palmer, as a young man of some ingenuity, though he
seriously expostulated with me upon the principles of my
pamphlet, which to him appeared abominable.   My printing
this pamphlet was another *erratum*.   While I lodged in
Little Britain, I made an acquaintance with one Wilcox,
a bookseller, whose shop was next door.   He had an immense
collection of second-hand books.   Circulating libraries were
not then in use; but we agreed, that, on certain reasonable
terms, which I have now forgotten, I might take, read, and
return any of his books.   This I esteemed a great advantage,
and I made as much use of it as I could.

My pamphlet by some means falling into the hands of one
Lyons, a surgeon, author of a book entitled, " *The Infallibility of Human Judgment*," it occasioned an acquaintance
between us.   He took great notice of me, called on me often
to converse on those subjects, carried me to the Horns, a pale
alehouse in —— Lane, Cheapside, and introduced me to Dr.
Mandeville, author of the " *Fable of the Bees*," who had a
club there, of which he was the soul; being a most facetious,
entertaining companion.   Lyons too introduced me to Dr.
Pemberton, at Batson's Coffee-house, who promised to give
me an opportunity, some time or other, of seeing Sir Isaac
Newton, of which I was extremely desirous; but this never
happened.

I had brought over a few curiosities, among which the principal was a purse made of the *asbestos*, which purifies by fire. Sir Hans Sloane heard of it, came to see me, and invited me to his house in Bloomsbury Square, showed me all his curiosities, and persuaded me to add that to the number; for which he paid me handsomely.

In our house lodged a young woman, a milliner, who, I think, had a shop in the Cloisters. She had been genteely bred, was sensible, lively, and of a most pleasing conversation. Ralph read plays to her in the evenings, they grew intimate, she took another lodging, and he followed her. They lived together some time; but, he being still out of business, and her income not sufficient to maintain them with her child, he took a resolution of going from London, to try for a country school, which he thought himself well qualified to undertake, as he wrote an excellent hand, and was a master of arithmetic and accounts. This, however, he deemed a business below him, and, confident of future better fortune, when he should be unwilling to have it known that he once was so meanly employed, he changed his name, and did me the honour to assume mine; for I soon after had a letter from him, acquainting me that he was settled in a small village (in Berkshire, I think it was, where he taught reading and writing to ten or a dozen boys, at sixpence each per week), recommending Mrs. T—— to my care, and desiring me to write to him, directing for *Mr. Franklin*, schoolmaster, at such a place.

He continued to write to me frequently, sending me large specimens of an epic poem, which he was then composing, and desiring my remarks and corrections. These I gave him from time to time, but endeavoured rather to discourage his proceeding. One of Young's Satires was then just published. I copied and sent him a great part of it, which set in a strong light the folly of pursuing the Muses. All was in vain; sheets of the poem continued to come by every post. In the mean time, Mrs. T——, having on his account lost her friends and business, was often in distresses, and used to send for me, and borrow what money I could spare to help to alleviate them. I grew fond of her company, and, being at that time under no religious restraint, and taking advantage of my importance to her, I attempted to take some liberties with her (another *erratum*), which she repulsed, with a proper degree of resentment. She wrote to Ralph and acquainted him with my conduct; this occasioned a breach between us; and, when he returned to London, he let me know he considered all the obligations he had been under to me as annulled; from which I concluded I was never to expect his repaying the money I had lent him, or that I had advanced for him. This, however, was of little consequence, as he was totally unable; and by the loss of his friendship I found myself relieved from a heavy burden. I now began to think of getting a little beforehand, and, expecting better employment, I left Palmer's to work at Watts's, near Lincoln's Inn Fields, a still greater printing-house. Here I continued all the rest of my stay in London.

At my first admission into the printing-house I took to working at press, imagining I felt a want of the bodily exercise I had been used to in America, where presswork is mixed with the composing. I drank only water; the other workmen, near fifty in number, were great drinkers of beer. On occasion I carried up and down stairs a large form of types in each hand, when others carried but one in both hands. They wondered to see, from this and several instances, that the *Water-American*, as they called me, was *stronger* than themselves, who drank *strong* beer! We had an alehouse boy, who attended always in the house to supply the workmen. My companion at the press drank every day a pint before breakfast, a pint at breakfast with his bread and cheese, a pint between breakfast and dinner, a pint at dinner, a pint in the afternoon about six o'clock, and another when he had done his day's work. I thought it a detestable custom; but it was necessary, he supposed, to drink *strong* beer that he might be *strong* to labour. I endeavoured to convince him, that the bodily strength afforded by beer could only be in proportion to the grain or flour of the barley dissolved in the water of which it was made; that there was more flour in a pennyworth of bread; and therefore, if he could eat that with a pint of water, it would give him more strength than a quart of beer. He drank on, however, and had four or five shillings to pay out of his wages every Saturday night for that vile liquor; an expense I was free from. And thus these poor devils keep themselves always under.

Watts, after some weeks, desiring to have me in the composing-room, I left the pressmen; a new *bien venu* for drink, being five shillings, was demanded of me by the compositors. I thought it an imposition, as I had paid one to the pressmen;

the master thought so too, and forbade my paying it. I stood out two or three weeks, was accordingly considered as an excommunicate, and had so many little pieces of private malice practised on me, by mixing my sorts, transposing and breaking my matter, &c. &c., if ever I stepped out of the room; and all ascribed to the *chapel ghost*, which they said ever haunted those not regularly admitted; that, notwithstanding the master's protection, I found myself obliged to comply and pay the money; convinced of the folly of being on ill terms with those one is to live with continually.

I was now on a fair footing with them, and soon acquired considerable influence. I proposed some reasonable alterations in their *chapel** laws, and carried them against all opposition. From my example, a great many of them left their muddling breakfast of beer, bread, and cheese, finding they could with me be supplied from a neighbouring house, with a large porringer of hot water-gruel, sprinkled with pepper, crumbled with bread, and a bit of butter in it, for the price of a pint of beer, viz. three halfpence. This was a more comfortable as well as a cheaper breakfast, and kept their heads clearer. Those, who continued sotting with their beer all day, were often, by not paying, out of credit at the alehouse, and used to make interest with me to get beer; their *light*, as they phrased it, *being out*. I watched the pay-table on Saturday night, and collected what I stood engaged for them, having to pay sometimes near thirty shillings a week on their accounts. This, and my being estimated a pretty good *riggite*, that is, a jocular verbal satirist, supported my consequence in the society. My constant attendance (I never making a *St. Monday*) recommended me to the master; and my uncommon quickness at composing occasioned my being put upon work of despatch, which was generally better paid. So I went on now very agreeably.

My lodgings in Little Britain being too remote, I found another in Duke Street, opposite to the Romish Chapel. It was up three pair of stairs backwards, at an Italian warehouse. A widow lady kept the house: she had a daughter, and a maid-servant, and a journeyman who attended the warehouse, but lodged abroad. After sending to inquire my character at the house where I last lodged, she agreed to take me in at the same rate—three shillings and sixpence a week; cheaper, as she said, from the protection she expected in having a man

* A printing-house is called a *chapel* by the workmen.

to lodge in the house. She was a widow, an elderly woman; had been bred a Protestant, being a clergyman's daughter, but was converted to the Catholic religion by her husband, whose memory she much revered; had lived much among people of distinction, and knew a thousand anecdotes of them as far back as the time of Charles II. She was lame in her knees with the gout, and therefore seldom stirred out of her room, so sometimes wanted company; and hers was so highly amusing to me, that I was sure to spend an evening with her whenever she desired it. Our supper was only half an anchovy each, on a very little slice of bread and butter, and half a pint of ale between us; but the entertainment was in her conversation. My always keeping good hours, and giving little trouble in the family, made her unwilling to part with me; so that when I talked of a lodging I had heard of, nearer my business, for two shillings a week (which, intent as I was on saving money, made some difference), she bid me not think of it, for she would abate me two shillings a week for the future: so I remained with her at one shilling and sixpence as long as I stayed in London.

In a garret of her house there lived a maiden lady of seventy, in the most retired manner, of whom my landlady gave me this account:—that she was a Roman Catholic; had been sent abroad when young, and lodged in a nunnery, with an intent of becoming a nun; but, the country not agreeing with her, she returned to England, where, there being no nunnery, she had vowed to lead the life of a nun, as near as might be done in those circumstances. Accordingly, she had given all her estate to charitable purposes, reserving only twelve pounds a year to live on; and out of this sum she still gave a part in charity, living herself on water-gruel only, and using no fire but to boil it. She had lived many years in that garret, being permitted to remain there gratis by successive Catholic tenants of the house below, as they deemed it a blessing to have her there. A priest visited her, to confess her every day. "From this I asked her," said my landlady, "how she, as she lived, could possibly find so much employment for a confessor?" "Oh!" said she, "it is impossible to avoid *vain thoughts.*" I was permitted once to visit her. She was cheerful and polite, and conversed pleasantly. The room was clean, but had no other furniture than a mattress, a table with a crucifix and a book, a stool which she gave me to sit on, and a picture over the chimney, of St. Veronica displaying her

handkerchief, with the miraculous figure of Christ's bleeding
face on it, which she explained to me with great seriousness.
She looked pale, but was never sick ; and I give it as another
instance, on how small an income life and health may be supported.

At Watts's printing-house I contracted an acquaintance
with an ingenious young man, one Wygate, who, having
wealthy relations, had been better educated than most printers ;
was a tolerable Latinist, spoke French, and loved reading. I
taught him and a friend of his to swim, at twice going into
the river, and they soon became good swimmers. They introduced me to some gentlemen from the country, who went to
Chelsea by water, to see the college and Don Saltero's curiosities. In our return, at the request of the company, whose
curiosity Wygate had excited, I stripped and leaped into the
river, and swam from near Chelsea to Blackfriars ; performing
in the way many feats of activity, both upon and under the
water, that surprised and pleased those to whom they were
novelties.

I had from a child been delighted with this exercise, had
studied and practised Thevenot's motions and positions, and
added some of my own, aiming at the graceful and easy as
well as the useful.* All these I took this occasion of exhibiting to the company, and was much flattered by their
admiration ; and Wygate, who was desirous of becoming a
master, grew more and more attached to me on that account,
as well as from the similarity of our studies. He at length
proposed to me travelling all over Europe together, supporting
ourselves everywhere by working at our business. I was once
inclined to it ; but mentioning it to my good friend Mr. Denham, with whom I often spent an hour when I had leisure, he
dissuaded me from it ; advising me to think only of returning
to Pennsylvania, which he was now about to do.

I must record one trait of this good man's character. He
had formerly been in business at Bristol, but failed in debt to
a number of people, compounded, and went to America.
There, by a close application to business as a merchant, he
acquired a plentiful fortune in a few years. Returning to
England in the ship with me, he invited his old creditors to
an entertainment, at which he thanked them for the easy
composition they had favoured him with ; and, when they
expected nothing but the treat, every man, at the first remove,

* He wrote two interesting papers on the art of swimming.—Ed.

found under his plate an order on a banker for the full amount of the unpaid remainder, with interest.

He now told me he was about to return to Philadelphia, and should carry over a great quantity of goods, in order to open a store there. He proposed to take me over as his clerk, to keep his books—in which he would instruct me—copy his letters, and attend the store. He added, that, as soon as I should be acquainted with mercantile business, he would promote me by sending me with a cargo of flour and bread to the West Indies, and procure me commissions from others which would be profitable; and, if I managed well, would establish me handsomely. The thing pleased me; for I was grown tired of London, remembered with pleasure the happy months I had spent in Pennsylvania, and wished again to see it. Therefore I immediately agreed, on the terms of fifty pounds a year, Pennsylvania money; less, indeed, than my then present gettings as a compositor, but affording a better prospect.

I now took leave of printing, as I thought, for ever, and was daily employed in my new business, going about with Mr. Denham among the tradesmen to purchase various articles, and see them packed up, delivering messages, calling upon workmen to despatch, &c.; and when all was on board, I had a few days' leisure. On one of these days, I was, to my surprise, sent for by a great man I knew only by name, Sir William Wyndham, and I waited upon him. He had heard by some means or other of my swimming from Chelsea to Blackfriars, and of my teaching Wygate and another young man to swim in a few hours. He had two sons, about to set out on their travels; he wished to have them first taught swimming, and proposed to gratify me handsomely if I would teach them. They were not yet come to town, and my stay was uncertain; so I could not undertake it. But from the incident I thought it likely, that if I were to remain in England, and open a swimming-school, I might get a good deal of money; and it struck me so strongly, that, had the overture been made me sooner, probably I should not so soon have returned to America. Many years after, you and I had something of more importance to do with one of these sons of Sir William Wyndham, become Earl of Egremont, which I shall mention in its place.

Thus I passed about eighteen months in London; most part of the time I worked hard at my business, and spent but little

upon myself except in seeing plays, and in books. My friend
Ralph had kept me poor; he owed me about twenty-seven
pounds, which I was now never likely to receive; a great sum
out of my small earnings! I loved him, notwithstanding, for
he had many amiable qualities. I had improved my know
ledge, however, though I had by no means improved my for
tune; but I had made some very ingenious acquaintance,
whose conversation was of great advantage to me; and I had
read considerably.

CHAPTER IV.

WE sailed from Gravesend on the 23rd of July, 1726. For
the incidents of the voyage, I refer you to my Journal,*
where you will find them all minutely related. Perhaps the
most important part of that journal is the *plan* † to be found
in it, which I formed at sea, for regulating the future conduct
of my life. It is the more remarkable, as being formed when
I was so young, and yet being pretty faithfully adhered to
quite through to old age.

We landed at Philadelphia the 11th of October, where I
found sundry alterations. Keith was no longer governor,
being superseded by Major Gordon; I met him walking the
streets as a common citizen. He seemed a little ashamed at
seeing me, and passed without saying anything. I should
have been as much ashamed at seeing Miss Read, had not her
friends, despairing with reason of my return, after the receipt
of my letter, persuaded her to marry another, one Rogers, a
potter, which was done in my absence. With him, however,
she was never happy, and soon parted from him, refusing to
cohabit with him or bear his name, it being now said he had
another wife. He was a worthless fellow, though an excellent
workman, which was the temptation to her friends. He got
into debt, ran away in 1727 or 1728, went to the West Indies,
and died there. Keimer had got a better house, a shop well
supplied with stationery, plenty of new types, and a number
of hands, though none good, and seemed to have a great deal
of business.

* This will be given in a future volume of the present series.—ED.

† This *plan* does not exist in the manuscript Journal found among
Dr. Franklin's papers; which appears, by a note thereon, to be a
"*copy made at Reading, in Pennsylvania. October 2nd, 1787.*"—W. T. F

Mr. Denham took a store in Water Street, where we opened our goods; I attended the business diligently, studied accounts, and grew in a little time expert at selling. We lodged and boarded together; he counselled me as a father, having a sincere regard for me. I respected and loved him, and we might have gone on together very happily; but, in the beginning of February, 1727, when I had just passed my twenty-first year, we both were taken ill. My distemper was a pleurisy, which very nearly carried me off. I suffered a good deal, gave up the point in my own mind, and was at the time rather disappointed when I found myself recovering; regretting, in some degree, that I must now, some time or other, have all that disagreeable work to go over again. I forget what Mr. Denham's distemper was; it held him a long time, and at length carried him off. He left me a small legacy in a nuncupative will, as a token of his kindness for me, and he left me once more to the wide world; for the store was taken into the care of his executors, and my employment under him ended.

My brother-in-law, Holmes, being now at Philadelphia, advised my return to my business; and Keimer tempted me, with an offer of large wages by the year, to come and take the management of his printing-house, that he might better attend to his stationer's shop. I had heard a bad character of him in London from his wife and her friends, and was not for having any more to do with him. I wished for employment as a merchant's clerk; but, not meeting with any, I closed again with Keimer. I found in his house these hands: Hugh Meredith, a Welsh Pennsylvanian, thirty years of age, bred to country work; he was honest, sensible, a man of experience, and fond of reading, but addicted to drinking. Stephen Potts, a young countryman of full age, bred to the same, of uncommon natural parts, and great wit and humour; but a little idle. These he had agreed with at extreme low wages per week, to be raised a shilling every three months, as they would deserve by improving in their business; and the expectation of these high wages, to come on hereafter, was what he had drawn them in with. Meredith was to work at press, Potts at bookbinding, which he by agreement was to teach them, though he knew neither one nor the other. John ——, a wild Irishman, brought up to no business, whose service, for four years, Keimer had purchased from the captain of a ship; he too was to be made a pressman

George Webb, an Oxford scholar, whose time for four years he had likewise bought, intending him for a compositor, of whom more presently; and David Harry, a country boy, whom he had taken apprentice.

I soon perceived that the intention of engaging me at wages so much higher than he had been used to give, was to have these raw cheap hands formed through me; and as soon as I had instructed them, they being all articled to him, he should be able to do without me. I went, however, very cheerfully, put his printing-house in order, which had been in great confusion, and brought his hands by degrees to mind their business and to do it better.

It was an odd thing to find an Oxford scholar in the situation of a bought servant. He was not more than eighteen years of age, and he gave me this account of himself; that he was born in Gloucester, educated at a grammar school, and had been distinguished among the scholars for some apparent superiority in performing his part when they exhibited plays; belonged to the Wits' Club there, and had written some pieces in prose and verse, which were printed in the Gloucester newspapers. Thence was sent to Oxford; there he continued about a year, but not well satisfied; wishing of all things to see London, and become a player. At length receiving his quarterly allowance of fifteen guineas, instead of discharging his debts, he went out of town, hid his gown in a furze bush, and walked to London; where, having no friend to advise him, he fell into bad company, soon spent his guineas, found no means of being introduced among the players, grew necessitous, pawned his clothes, and wanted bread. Walking the street very hungry, not knowing what to do with himself, a crimp's bill was put into his hand, offering immediate entertainment and encouragement to such as would bind themselves to serve in America. He went directly, signed the indentures, was put into the ship, and came over; never writing a line to his friends to acquaint them what was become of him. He was lively, witty, good-natured, and a pleasant companion; but idle, thoughtless, and imprudent to the last degree.

John, the Irishman, soon ran away; with the rest I began to live very agreeably, for they all respected me the more, as they found Keimer incapable of instructing them, and that from me they learned something daily. My acquaintance with ingenious people in the town increased. We never worked on Saturday, that being Keimer's Sabbath, so that I had two days for reading. Keimer himself treated me with great civility and apparent regard, and nothing now made me uneasy but my debt to Vernon, which I was yet unable to pay, being hitherto but a poor economist. He, however, kindly made no demand of it.

Our printing-house often wanted sorts, and there was no letter-foundry in America; I had seen types cast at James's in London, but without much attention to the manner; however, I contrived a mould, and made use of the letters we had as puncheons, struck the matrixes in lead, and thus supplied in a pretty tolerable way all deficiencies. I also engraved several things on occasion; made the ink; I was warehouse-man; and, in short, quite a *fac-totum*.

But, however serviceable I might be, I found that my services became every day of less importance, as the other hands improved in their business; and, when Keimer paid me a second quarter's wages, he let me know that he felt them too heavy, and thought I should make an abatement. He grew by degrees less civil, put on more the airs of master, frequently found fault, was captious, and seemed ready for an outbreaking. I went on nevertheless with a good deal of patience, thinking that his incumbered circumstances were partly the cause. At length a trifle snapped our connexion; for, a great noise happening near the court-house, I put my head out of the window to see what was the matter. Keimer, being in the street, looked up and saw me, called out to me in a loud voice and angry tone to mind my business; adding some reproachful words, that nettled me the more for their publicity; all the neighbours who were looking out on the same occasion being witnesses how I was treated. He came up immediately into the printing-house; continued the quarrel, high words passed on both sides, he gave me the quarter's warning we had stipulated, expressing a wish that he had not been obliged to so long a warning. I told him his wish was unnecessary, for I would leave him that instant; and so taking my hat walked out of doors, desiring Meredith, whom I saw below, to take care of some things I left, and bring them to my lodgings.

Meredith came accordingly in the evening, when we talked my affair over. He had conceived a great regard for me, and was very unwilling that I should leave the house while he remained in it. He dissuaded me from returning to my native country, which I began to think of; he reminded me that Keimer was in debt for all he possessed, that his creditors began to be uneasy; that he kept his shop miserably, sold often without a profit for ready money, and often trusted without keeping accounts; that he must therefore fail, which would make a vacancy I might profit of. I objected my want of money. He then let me know that his father had a high opinion of me, and, from some discourse that had passed between them, he was sure would advance money to set me up, if I would enter into partnership with him. "My time," said he, "will be out with Keimer in the spring; by that time we may have our press and types in from London. I am sensible I am no workman; if you like it, your skill in the business shall be set against the stock I furnish, and we will share the profits equally."

The proposal was agreeable to me, and I consented; his father was in town, and approved of it; the more as he said I had great influence with his son, had prevailed on him to abstain long from dram-drinking, and he hoped might break him of that wretched habit entirely, when we came to be so closely connected. I gave an inventory to the father, who carried it to a merchant; the things were sent for, the secret was to be kept till they should arrive, and in the meantime I was to get work, if I could, at the other printing-house. But I found no vacancy there, and so remained idle a few days, when Keimer, on a prospect of being employed to print some paper money in New Jersey, which would require cuts and various types that I only could supply, and apprehending Bradford might engage me and get the job from him, sent me a very civil message, that old friends should not part for a few words, the effect of sudden passion, and wishing me to return. Meredith persuaded me to comply, as it would give more opportunity for his improvement under my daily instructions; so I returned, and we went on more smoothly than for some time before. The New Jersey job was obtained; I contrived a copper-plate press for it, the first that had been seen in the country; I cut several ornaments and checks for the bills. We went together to Burlington, where I executed the whole to satisfaction; and he received so large a sum for the work, as to be enabled thereby to keep himself longer from ruin.

At Burlington I made acquaintance with many principal people of the province. Several of them had been appointed by the Assembly a committee to attend the press, and take care that no more bills were printed than the law directed. They 'were, therefore, by turns constantly with us, and generally he who attended brought with him a friend or two for company. My mind having been much more improved by reading than Keimer's, I suppose it was for that reason my conversation seemed to be more valued. They had me to their houses, introduced me to their friends, and showed me much civility; while he, though the master, was a little neglected. In truth, he was an odd creature; ignorant of common life, fond of rudely opposing received opinions, slovenly to extreme dirtiness, enthusiastic in some points of religion, and a little knavish withal.

We continued there near three months; and by that time I could reckon among my acquired friends, Judge Allen, Samuel Bustill, the Secretary of the Province, Isaac Pearson, Joseph Cooper, and several of the Smiths, members of Assembly, and Isaac Decow, the Surveyor-General. The latter was a shrewd, sagacious old man, who told me, that he began for himself, when young, by wheeling clay for the brickmakers; learned to write after he was of age; carried the chain for surveyors, who taught him surveying, and he had now, by his industry, acquired a good estate; and said he, " I foresee that you will soon work this man out of his business, and make a fortune in it at Philadelphia." He had then not the least intimation of my intention to set up there or anywhere. These friends were afterwards of great use to me, as I occasionally was to some of them. They all continued their regard for me as long as they lived.

Before I enter upon my public appearance in business, it may be well to let you know the then state of my mind, with regard to my principles and morals, that you may see how far those influenced the future events of my life. My parents had early given me religious impressions, and brought me through my childhood piously in the Dissenting way. But I was scarce fifteen, when, after doubting by turns several points, as I found them disputed in the different books I read, I began to doubt of the Revelation itself. Some books against Deism fell into my hands; they were said to be the substance of the sermons, which had been preached at Boyle's Lectures. It happened, that they wrought an effect on me quite contrary to what was intended by them. For the arguments of the Deists, which were quoted to be refuted, appeared to me much stronger than the refutations; in short, I soon became a thorough Deist. My arguments perverted some others, particularly Collins and Ralph; but, each of these having wronged me greatly without the least compunction, and recollecting Keith's conduct towards me, (who was another freethinker,) and my own towards Vernon and Miss Read, which at times gave me great trouble. I began to suspect that this doctrine, though it might be true, was not very useful. My London pamphlet, printed in 1725*, which had for its motto these lines of Dryden;

> "Whatever is, is right. But purblind man
> Sees but a part o' the chain, the nearest links;
> His eyes not carrying to that equal beam,
> That poises all above;"

and which from the attributes of God, his infinite wisdom, goodness, and power, concluded that nothing could possibly be wrong in the world; and that vice and virtue were empty distinctions, no such things existing; appeared now not so clever a performance as I once thought it; and I doubted

---

* Dr. Franklin, in a letter to Benjamin Vaughan, dated November 9th, 1779, gives a further account of this pamphlet in these words:—

"It was addressed to Mr. J. R., that is, James Ralph, then a youth of about my age, and my intimate friend; afterwards a political writer and historian. The purport of it was to prove the doctrine of fate, from the supposed attributes of God; in some such manner as this. That in erecting and governing the world, as he was infinitely wise, he knew what would be best; infinitely good, he must be disposed, and infinitely powerful, he must be able to execute it. Consequently *all is right*.

"There were only a hundred copies printed, of which I gave a few to friends; and afterwards disliking the piece, as conceiving it might have an ill tendency, I burnt the rest, except one copy, the margin of which was filled with manuscript notes by Lyons, author of the *Infallibility of Human Judgment*, who was at that time another of my acquaintance in London. I was not nineteen years of age when it was written. In 1730, I wrote a piece on the other side of the question. which began with laying for its foundation this fact; ' *That almost all men in all ages and countries have at times made use of* PRAYER.' Thence I reasoned, that, if all things are ordained, prayer must among the rest be ordained. But, as prayer can procure no change in things that are ordained, praying must then be useless, and an absurdity. God would therefore not ordain praying, if everything else was ordained. But praying exists, therefore all other things are not ordained, &c. This pamphlet was never printed, and the manuscript has been long lost. The great uncertainty I found in metaphysical reasonings disgusted me, and I quitted that kind of reading and study for others more satisfactory."—W. T. F.

whether some error had not insinuated itself unperceived into my argument so as to infect all that followed, as is common in metaphysical reasonings.

I grew convinced that *truth, sincerity*, and *integrity*, in dealings between man and man, were of the utmost importance to the felicity of life ; and I formed written resolutions, which still remain in my journal book, to practise them ever while I lived.* Revelation had indeed no weight with me,

* See *Articles of Belief and Acts of Religion*, published in his works.
Among Franklin's papers I have found a curious manuscript in his handwriting, which contains a new version of the Lord's Prayer. The condition and appearance of the manuscript prove it to have been an early performance, but its precise date is not known. The form in which it is written is here preserved.—Ee.

THE LORD'S PRAYER.

OLD VERSION.	NEW VERSION, BY B. FRANKLIN.
1. Our Father which art in heaven,	1. Heavenly Father,
2. Hallowed be thy name.	2. May all revere thee,
3. Thy kingdom come,	3. And become thy dutiful children and faithful subjects.
4. Thy will be done on earth, as it is in heaven.	4. May thy laws be obeyed on earth, as perfectly as they are in heaven.
5. Give us this day our daily bread.	5. Provide for us this day, as thou hast hitherto daily done.
6. Forgive us our debts as we forgive our debtors.	6. Forgive us our trespasses, and enable us to forgive those who offend us.
4. And lead us not into temptation, bu deliver us from evil.	7. Keep us out of temptation, and deliver us from evil.

REASONS FOR THE CHANGE OF EXPRESSION.

OLD VERSION.—*Our Father which art in Heaven.*

NEW VERSION.—*Heavenly Father* is more concise, equally expressive, and better modern English.

OLD VERSION.—*Hallowed be thy name.* This seems to relate to an observance among the Jews not to pronounce the proper or peculiar name of God, they deeming it a prophanation so to do. We have in our language no *proper name* for God ; the word *God* being a common, or general name, expressing all chief objects of worship, true or false. The word *hallowed* is almost obsolete. People now have but an imperfect conception of the meaning of the petition. It is therefore proposed to change the expression into

NEW VERSION.— *May all revere thee.*

OLD VERSION.—*Thy kingdom come.* This petition seems suited to the then condition of the Jewish nation. Originally their state was a theocracy; God was their king. Dissatisfied with that kind of government, they desired a visible, earthly king, in the manner of the nations around them. They had such kings accordingly; but their

as such; but I entertained an opinion, that, though certain
actions might not be bad, *because* they were forbidden by it,
or good, *because* it commanded them; yet probably those
actions might be forbidden *because* they were bad for us, or
commanded *because* they were beneficial to us, in their own
natures, all the circumstances of things considered.   And this
persuasion, with the kind hand of Providence, or some guar-
dian angel, or accidental favourable circumstances and situations, or all together, preserved me, through this dangerous
time of youth, and the hazardous situations I was sometimes
in among strangers, remote from the eye and advice of my
father, free from any *wilful* gross immorality or injustice,
that might have been expected from my want of religion.   I
say *wilful*, because the instances I have mentioned had something of *necessity* in them, from my youth, inexperience, and
the knavery of others.   I had therefore a tolerable character
to begin the world with; I valued it properly, and determined
to preserve it.

We had not been long returned to Philadelphia, before the
happiness was not increased by the change, and they had reason to
wish and pray for a return of the theocracy, or government of God.
Christians in these times have other ideas, when they speak of the kingdom of God, such as are perhaps more adequately expressed by the

NEW VERSION.—*Become thy dutiful children and faithful subjects.*

OLD VERSION.—*Thy will be done on earth, as it is in heaven ;* more
explicitly,

NEW VERSION.—*May thy laws be obeyed on earth, as perfectly as they
are in heaven.*

OLD VERSION.—*Give us this day our daily bread.*—Give us what is
ours seems to put in a claim of right, and to contain too little of the
grateful acknowledgment and sense of dependence that become
creatures, who live on the daily bounty of their Creator.   Therefore it
is changed to

NEW VERSION.—*Provide for us this day, as thou hast hitherto daily
done.*

OLD VERSION.—*Forgive us our debts, as we forgive our debtors.*
(Matthew).   *Forgive us our sins, for we also forgive every one that is
indebted to us.*   (Luke).   Offerings were *due* to God on many occasions
by the Jewish law, which, when people could not pay, or had forgotten,
as debtors are apt to do, it was proper to pray that those debts might be
forgiven.   Our Liturgy uses neither the *debtors* of Matthew, nor the *in
debted* of Luke, but instead of them speaks of *those that trespass against
us.*   Perhaps the considering it as a Christian duty to forgive debtors
was by the compilers thought an inconvenient idea in a trading nation.
There seems, however, something presumptuous in this mode of expression, which has the air of proposing ourselves as an example of goodness fit for God to imitate.   *We hope you will at least be as good as we*

new types arrived from London. We settled with Keimer, and left him by his consent before he heard of it. We found a house to let near the Market, and took it. To lessen the rent, which was then but twenty-four pounds a year, though I have since known it let for seventy, we took in Thomas Godfrey, a glazier, and his family, who were to pay a considerable part of it to us, and we to board with them. We had scarce opened our letters, and put our press in order, before George House, an acquaintance of mine, brought a countryman to us, whom he had met in the street, inquiring for a printer. All our cash was now expended in the variety of particulars we had been obliged to procure, and this country-man's five shillings, being our first-fruits, and coming so seasonably, gave me more pleasure than any crown I have since earned; and the gratitude I felt towards House has made me often more ready, than perhaps I otherwise should have been, to assist young beginners.

There are croakers in every country, always boding its ruin. Such an one there lived in Philadelphia; a person of note, an elderly man, with a wise look, and a very grave manner of speaking; his name was Samuel Mickle. This gentleman, a stranger to me, stopped me one day at my door, and asked me if I was the young man who had lately opened a new printing-house? Being answered in the affirmative, he said he was sorry for me, because it was an expensive undertaking, and

are; you see we forgive one another, and therefore we pray that you would forgive us. Some have considered it in another sense. *Forgive us as we forgive others.* That is, if we do not forgive others, we pray that thou wouldst not forgive us. But this, being a kind of conditional *imprecation* against ourselves, seems improper in such a prayer; and therefore it may be better to say humbly and modestly,

NEW VERSION.—*Forgive us our trespasses, and enable us likewise to forgive those who offend us.* This, instead of assuming that we have already in and of ourselves the grace of forgiveness, acknowledges our dependence on God, the Fountain of Mercy, for any share we may have of it, praying that he would communicate it to us.

OLD VERSION.—*And lead us not into temptation.* The Jews had a notion, that God sometimes tempted, or directed, or permitted, the tempting of people. Thus it was said, he tempted Pharaoh, directed Satan to tempt Job, and a false Prophet to tempt Ahab. Under this persuasion, it was natural for them to pray, that he would not put them to such severe trials. We now suppose that temptation, so far as it is supernatural, comes from the Devil only; and this petition continued conveys a suspicion, which, in our present conceptions, seems unworthy of God: therefore it might be altered to

NEW VERSION.—*Keep us out of temptation.*

the expense would be lost; for Philadelphia was a sinking place, the people already half bankrupts, or near being so; all the appearances of the contrary, such as new buildings and the rise of rents, being to his certain knowledge fallacious; for they were in fact among the things that would ruin us. Then he gave me such a detail of misfortunes now existing, or that were soon to exist, that he left me half melancholy. Had I known him before I engaged in this business, probably I never should have done it. This person continued to live in this decaying place, and to declaim in the same strain, refusing for many years to buy a house there, because all was going to destruction; and at last I had the pleasure of seeing him give five times as much for one, as he might have bought it for when he first began croaking.

CHAPTER V.

I SHOULD have mentioned before, that in the autumn of the preceding year I had formed most of my ingenious acquaintance into a club for mutual improvement, which we called the JUNTO. We met on Friday evenings. The rules that I drew up required that every member, in his turn, should produce one or more queries on any point of Morals, Politics, or Natural Philosophy, to be discussed by the company; and once in three months produce and read an essay of his own writing, on any subject he pleased. Our debates were to be under the direction of a president, and to be conducted in the sincere spirit of inquiry after truth, without fondness for dispute, or desire of victory; and, to prevent warmth, all expressions of positiveness in opinions, or direct contradiction, were after some time made contraband, and prohibited under small pecuniary penalties.

The first members were Joseph Breintnal, a copier of deeds for the scriveners, a good-natured, friendly, middle-aged man, a great lover of poetry, reading all he could meet with, and writing some that was tolerable; very ingenious in making little nicknackeries, and of sensible conversation.

Thomas Godfrey, a self-taught mathematician, great in his way, and afterwards inventor of what is now called *Hadley's Quadrant.** But he knew little out of his way, and was not

* Godfrey's claims to this invention are fully explained and con-

a pleasing companion; as, like most great mathematicians I have met with, he expected universal precision in everything said, or was for ever denying or distinguishing upon trifles, to the disturbance of all conversation. He soon left us.

Nicholas Scull, a surveyor, afterwards surveyor-general, who loved books, and sometimes made a few verses.

William Parsons, bred a shoemaker, but loving reading had acquired a considerable share of mathematics, which he first studied with a view to astrology, and afterwards laughed at it. He also became surveyor-general.

William Maugridge, joiner, but a most exquisite mechanic, and a solid, sensible man.

Hugh Meredith, Stephen Potts, and George Webb, I have characterized before.

Robert Grace, a young gentleman of some fortune, generous, lively, and witty; a lover of punning and of his friends.

Lastly, William Coleman, then a merchant's clerk, about my age, who had the coolest, clearest head, the best heart, and the exactest morals, of almost any man I ever met with. He became afterwards a merchant of great note, and one of our provincial judges. Our friendship continued without interruption to his death, upwards of forty years; and the club continued almost as long, and was the best school of philosophy, morality, and politics, that then existed in the province; for our queries, which were read the week preceding their discussion, put us upon reading with attention on the several subjects, that we might speak more to the purpose; and here, too, we acquired better habits of conversation, everything being studied in our rules which might prevent our disgusting each other. Hence the long continuance of the club, which I shall have frequent occasion to speak further of hereafter.

But my giving this account of it here, is to show something of the interest I had. every one of these exerting themselves in recommending business to us. Breintnal particularly procured us from the Quakers the printing of forty sheets of their history, the rest being to be done by Keimer; and upon these we worked exceedingly hard, for the price was low. It was a folio, *pro patriâ* size, in pica, with long primer notes. I composed a sheet a day, and Meredith worked it off at press. It was often eleven at night, and sometimes later, before I

firmed in MILLER's *Retrospect of the Eighteenth Centnry*, Vol. L pp. 468—480.

had finished my distribution for the next day's work; for the little jobs sent in by our other friends now and then put us back. But so determined I was to continue doing a sheet a day of the folio, that one night, when having imposed my forms I thought my day's work over, one of them by accident was broken, and two pages reduced to *pie.* I immediately distributed and composed it over again before I went to bed; and this industry, visible to our neighbours, began to give us character and credit. Particularly I was told, that mention being made of the new printing-office, at the merchants' every-night club, the general opinion was that it must fail, there being already two printers in the place, Keimer and Bradford. But Dr. Baird (whom you and I saw many years after at his native place, St. Andrew's, in Scotland) gave a contrary opinion; "For the industry of that Franklin," said he, "is superior to anything I ever saw of the kind. I see him still at work when I go home from club, and he is at work again before his neighbours are out of bed." This struck the rest, and we soon after had offers from one of them to supply us with stationery; but as yet we did not choose to engage in shop business.

I mention this industry more particularly and the more freely, though it seems to be talking in my own praise, that those of my posterity who shall read it, may know the use of that virtue, when they see its effects in my favour throughout this relation.

George Webb, who had found a female friend that lent him wherewith to purchase his time of Keimer, now came to offer himself as a journeyman to us. We could not then employ him; but I foolishly let him know, as a secret, that I soon intended to begin a newspaper, and might then have work for him. My hopes of success, as I told him, were founded on this; that the then only newspaper, printed by Bradford, was a paltry thing, wretchedly managed, no way entertaining, and yet was profitable to him,—I therefore freely thought a good paper would scarcely fail of good encouragement. I requested Webb not to mention it; but he told it to Keimer, who immediately, to be beforehand with me, published proposals for one himself, on which Webb was to be employed. I was vexed at this; and to counteract them, not being able to commence our paper, I wrote several amusing pieces for Bradford's paper, under the title of THE BUSY BODY, which Breintnal continued some months. By this means the attention of the public was fixed on that paper; and Keimer's proposals, which we burlesqued and ridiculed, were disregarded. He began his paper, however; and before carrying it on three quarters of a year, with at most only ninety subscribers, he offered it me for a trifle; and I, having been ready some time to go on with it, took it in hand directly, and it proved in a few years extremely profitable to me.*

I perceive that I am apt to speak in the singular number though our partnership still continued; it may be, that in fact the whole management of the business lay upon me. Meredith was no compositor, a poor pressman, and seldom sober. My friends lamented my connexion with him, but I was to make the best of it.

Our first papers made quite a different appearance from any before in the province; a better type and better printed; but some remarks† of my writing, on the dispute then going on

---

* It was called the *Pennsylvania Gazette.* Franklin and Meredith began the paper with No. 40, September 25th, 1729.

A characteristic anecdote has been related of Franklin, illustrative of his independence as an editor. Soon after the establishment of his newspaper, he found occasion to remark with some degree of freedom on the public conduct of one or two persons of high standing in Philadelphia. This course was disapproved by some of his patrons, who sought an opportunity to convey to him their views of the subject, and what they represented to be the opinion of his friends. He listened patiently, and replied by requesting that they would favour him with their company at supper, and bring with them the other gentlemen, who had expressed dissatisfaction. The time arrived, and the guests assembled. He received them cordially, and listened again to their friendly reproofs of his editorial conduct. At length supper was announced; but when the guests had seated themselves around the table, they were surprised to see nothing before them but two puddings, made of coarse meal, called *sawdust puddings* in the common phrase, and a stone pitcher filled with water. He helped them all, and then applied himself to his own plate, partaking freely of the repast, and urging his friends to do the same. They taxed their politeness to the utmost, but all in vain; their appetites refused obedience to the will. Perceiving their difficulty, Franklin at last arose and said, "*My friends, any one who can subsist upon sawdust pudding and water, as I can, needs no man's patronage.*"—ED.

† These remarks are in the *Pennsylvania Gazette* for October 2nd, 1729, and are as follows.

"His Excellency, Governor Burnet, died unexpectedly about two days after the date of this reply to his last message; and it was thought the dispute would have ended with him, or at least have lain dormant till the arrival of a new Governor from England, who possibly might, or might not, be inclined to enter too vigorously into the measures of his between Governor Burnet and the Massachusetts Assembly, struck the principal people, occasioned the paper and the manager of it to be much talked of, and in a few weeks brought them all to be our subscribers.

Their example was followed by many, and our number went on growing continually. This was one of the first good effects of my having learned a little to scribble; another was, that the leading men, seeing a newspaper now in the hands of those who could also handle a pen, thought it convenient to oblige and encourage me. Bradford still printed the votes,

predecessor. But our last advices by the post acquaint us, that his Honour, the Lieutenant-Governor, on whom the government immediately devolves upon the death or absence of the Commander-in-Chief, has vigorously renewed the struggle on his own account, of which the particulars will be seen in our next.

" Perhaps some of our readers may not fully understand the original ground of this warm contest between the Governor and Assembly. It seems *that* people have for these hundred years past enjoyed the privilege of rewarding the Governor for the time being, according to *their sense* of his merit and services; and few or none of their Governors have complained, or had cause to complain, of a scanty allowance. When the late Governor Burnet brought with him instructions to demand a *settled salary* of one thousand pounds sterling per annum, on him and all his successors, and the Assembly were required to fix it immediately, he insisted on it strenuously to the last, and they as constantly refused it. It appears by their votes and proceedings, that they thought it an imposition, contrary to their own charter, and to *Magna Charta;* and they judged that there should be a mutual dependence between the *Governor* and *governed;* and that to make the Governor independent would be dangerous and destructive to their liberties, and the ready way to establish tyranny. They thought, likewise, that the province was not the less dependent on the Crown of Great Britain, by the Governor's depending immediately on them and his own good conduct for an ample support; because all acts and laws, which he might be induced to pass, must nevertheless be constantly sent home for approbation in order to continue in force. Many other reasons were given, and arguments used, in the course of the controversy, needless to particularize here, because all the material papers relating to it have been already given in our public news.

" Much deserved praise has the deceased Governor received for his steady integrity in adhering to his instructions, notwithstanding the great difficulty and opposition he met with, and the strong temptations offered from time to time to induce him to give up the point. And yet, perhaps, something is due to the Assembly, (as the love and zeal of that country for the present establishment is too well known to suffer any suspicion of want of loyalty,) who continue thus resolutely to abide by what *they think* their right, and that of the people they represent; maugré all the arts and menaces of a Governor famed for his cunning

and laws, and other public business. He had printed an
address of the House to the Governor, in a coarse blundering
manner; we reprinted it elegantly and correctly, and sent
one to every member. They were sensible of the difference,
it strengthened the hands of our friends in the House, and
they voted us their printers for the year ensuing.

Among my friends in the House I must not forget Mr.
Hamilton, before mentioned, who was then returned from
England, and had a seat in it. He interested himself for me
strongly in that instance, as he did in many others afterwards, continuing his patronage till his death*.

Mr. Vernon, about this time, put me in mind of the debt
I owed him, but did not press me. I wrote to him an in-
genuous letter of acknowledgment, craving his forbearance a
little longer, which he allowed me. As soon as I was able, I
paid the principal with the interest, and many thanks; so
that *erratum* was in some degree corrected†.

But now another difficulty came upon me, which I had
never the least reason to expect. Mr. Meredith's father, who
was to have paid for our printing-house, according to the
expectations given me, was able to advance only one hundred
pounds currency, which had been paid; and a hundred more
were due to the merchant, who grew impatient and sued us
all. We gave bail, but saw that if the money could not be
raised in time, the suit must soon come to a judgment and
execution, and our hopeful prospects must with us be ruined,
as the press and letters must be sold for payment, perhaps
at half price.

and politics, backed with instructions from home, and powerfully aided
by the great advantage such an officer always has of engaging the principal men of a place in his party, by conferring where he pleases so many
posts of profit and honour. Their happy mother country will perhaps
observe with pleasure, that though her gallant cocks and matchless dogs
abate their natural fire and intrepidity, when transported to a foreign
clime, (as this nation is,) yet her sons in the remotest part of the earth,
and even to the third and fourth descent, still retain that ardent spirit
of liberty, and that undaunted courage, which have in every age so
gloriously distinguished Britons and Englishmen from the rest of mankind."—W. T. F.

* I afterwards obtained for his son *five hundred pounds.*

† Many years afterwards he had an opportunity of discharging more
completely this debt of gratitude. While he was minister plenipotentiary from the United States at the court of France, he rendered very
important services to a young man, a descendant of Mr. Vernon, who
passed some time in that country.—Ed.

In this distress two true friends, whose kindness I have never forgotten, nor ever shall forget while I can remember anything, came to me separately, unknown to each other; and, without any application from me, offered each of them to advance me all the money that should be necessary to enable me to take the whole business upon myself, if that should be practicable; but they did not like my continuing the partnership with Meredith, who, as they said, was often seen drunk in the street, playing at low games in alehouses, much to our discredit. These two friends were William Coleman and Robert Grace. I told them I could not propose a separation, while any prospect remained of the Merediths' fulfilling their part of our agreement, because I thought myself under great obligations to them for what they had done, and would do if they could; but if they finally failed in their performance, and our partnership must be dissolved, I should then think myself at liberty to accept the assistance of my friends.

Thus the matter rested for some time, when I said to my partner, " Perhaps your father is dissatisfied at the part you have undertaken in this affair of ours, and is unwilling to advance for you and me what he would for you. If that is the case tell me, and I will resign the whole to you, and go about my business." " No," said he, " my father has really been disappointed, and is really unable, and I am unwilling to distress him further. I see this is a business I am not fit for. I was bred a farmer, and it was folly in me to come to town and put myself, at thirty years of age, an apprentice to learn a new trade. Many of our Welsh people are going to settle in North Carolina, where land is cheap. I am inclined to go with them, and follow my old employment; you may find friends to assist you. If you will take the debts of the company upon you, return to my father the hundred pounds he has advanced, pay my little personal debts, and give me thirty pounds and a new saddle, I will relinquish the partnership and leave the whole in your hands." I agreed to this proposal; it was drawn up in writing, signed, and sealed immediately. I gave him what he demanded, and he went soon after to Carolina; whence he sent me next year two long letters, containing the best account that had been given of that country, the climate, the soil, and husbandry, for in those matters he was very judicious. I printed them in the papers, and they gave great satisfaction to the public.

As soon as he was gone I recurred to my two friends, and because I would not give an unkind preference to either, I took half of what each had offered and I wanted of one, and half of the other; paid off the company's debts, and went on with the business in my own name, advertising that the partnership was dissolved. I think this was in or about the year 1729.*

About this time there was a cry among the people for more paper-money; only fifteen thousand pounds being extant in the province, and that soon to be sunk. The wealthy inhabitants opposed any addition, being against all paper currency, from the apprehension that it would depreciate as it had done in New England, to the injury of all creditors. We had discussed this point in our Junto, where I was on the side of an addition, being persuaded that the first small sum struck in 1723, had done much good by increasing the trade, employment, and number of inhabitants in the province, since I now saw all the old houses inhabited, and many new ones building; whereas I remembered well, when I first walked about the streets of Philadelphia, eating my roll, I saw many of the houses in Walnut Street, between Second and Front Streets, with bills on their doors, " *To be let,*" and many likewise in Chestnut Street and other streets, which made me think the inhabitants of the city were, one after another, deserting it.

Our debates possessed me so fully of the subject, that I wrote and printed an anonymous pamphlet on it, entitled, *The Nature and Necessity of a Paper Currency.*† It was well

---

* The dissolution of the partnership was a year later, as appears by the following agreement, transcribed from the original in Franklin's handwriting.—ED.

" Be it remembered, that Hugh Meredith and Benjamin Franklin have this day separated as partners, and will henceforth act each on his own account; and that the said Hugh Meredith, for a valuable consideration by him received from the said Benjamin Franklin, hath relinquished, and doth hereby relinquish, to the said Franklin, all claim, right, or property to or in the printing materials and stock heretofore jointly possessed by them in partnership; and to all debts due to them as partners, in the course of their business; which are all from henceforth the sole property of the said Benjamin Franklin. In witness whereof I have hereunto set my hand, this 14th day of July, 1730.

                " HUGH MEREDITH."

† " It is little known, or set down to the commendation of Franklin, that, when he was young in business, and stood in need of sundry articles in the line of his profession as a printer, he had the ingenuity to make them for himself. In this way he founded letters of lead, en-

received by the common people in general; but the rich men disliked it, for it increased and strengthened the clamour for more money; and, they happening to have no writers among them that were able to answer it, their opposition slackened, and the point was carried by a majority in the House. My friends there, who considered I had been of some service, thought fit to reward me, by employing me in printing the money; a very profitable job, and a great help to me. This was another advantage gained by my being able to write.

The utility of this currency became by time and experience so evident, that the principles upon which it was founded were never afterwards much disputed; so that it grew soon to fifty-five thousand pounds; and in 1739, to eighty thousand pounds; trade, building, and inhabitants all the while increasing. Though I now think there are limits, beyond which the quantity may be hurtful.

I soon after obtained, through my friend Hamilton, the printing of the Newcastle paper money, another profitable job, as I then thought it; small things appearing great to those in small circumstances; and these to me were really great advantages, as they were great encouragements. Mr. Hamilton procured for me also the printing of the laws and votes of that government; which continued in my hands as long as I followed the business.

I now opened a small stationer's shop. I had in it blanks

graved various printing ornaments, cut wood-cuts, made printer's ink, engraved copperplate vignettes, and made his plate-press.''—WATSON's *Annals of Philadelphia*, p. 513.

Mr. Watson relates another anecdote. He says, that the "yellow willow tree," now so common throughout the country, was first introduced into America by Franklin. A wicker basket made of willow, in which some foreign article had been imported, he saw sprouting in a ditch, and directed some of the twigs to be planted. They took root and from these shoots are supposed to have sprung all the yellow willows, which have grown on this side of the Atlantic.

Chaptal ascribes to Franklin, also, the introduction of the agricultural use of plaster of Paris into the United States. "As this celebrated philosopher," says he, "wished that the effects of this manure should strike the gaze of all cultivators, he wrote in great letters, formed by the use of the ground plaster, in a field of clover lying upon the great road, ' *This has been plastered.*' The prodigious vegetation, which was developed in the plastered portion, led him to adopt this method. Volumes upon the excellency of plaster would not have produced so speedy a revolution. From that period the Americans have imported great quantities of plaster of Paris."—CHAPTAL's *Agricultural Chemistry,* Boston edition, p. 73.—ED.

of all kinds; the correctest that ever appeared among us. I
was assisted in that by my friend Breintnal. I had also
paper, parchment, chapmen's books, &c. One Whitemarsh, a
compositor I had known in London, an excellent workman,
now came to me, and worked with me constantly and diligently; and I took an apprentice, the son of Aquila Rose.

I began now gradually to pay off the debt I was under for
the printing-house. In order to secure my credit and character as a tradesman, I took care not only to be in *reality*
industrious and frugal, but to avoid the appearances to the
contrary. I dressed plain, and was seen at no places of idle
diversion. I never went out a fishing or shooting; a book
indeed sometimes debauched me from my work, but that was
seldom, was private, and gave no scandal; and, to show that
I was not above my business, I sometimes brought home the
paper I purchased at the stores, through the streets on a
wheelbarrow. Thus being esteemed an industrious, thriving
young man, and paying duly for what I bought, the merchants who imported stationery solicited my custom; others
proposed supplying me with books, and I went on prosper-
ously. In the mean time, Keimer's credit and business declining daily, he was at last forced to sell his printing-house,
to satisfy his creditors. He went to Barbadoes, and there
lived some years in very poor circumstances.

His apprentice, David Harry, whom I had instructed while
I worked with him, set up in his place at Philadelphia, having bought his materials. I was at first apprehensive of a
powerful rival in Harry, as his friends were very able, and
had a good deal of interest. I therefore proposed a partnership to him, which he fortunately for me rejected with scorn.
He was very proud, dressed like a gentleman, lived expen-
sively, took much diversion and pleasure abroad, ran in debt,
and neglected his business; upon which, all business left
him; and, finding nothing to do, he followed Keimer to Barbadoes, taking the printing-house with him. There this apprentice employed his former master as a journeyman; they
quarrelled often, and Harry went continually behindhand,
and at length was obliged to sell his types and return to
country work in Pennsylvania. The person who bought
them employed Keimer to use them, but a few years after he
died.

There remained now no other printer in Philadelphia, but
the old Bradford; but he was rich and easy, did a little in

the business by straggling hands, but was not anxious about it. However, as he held the post-office, it was imagined he had better opportunities of obtaining news, his paper was thought a better distributer of advertisements than mine, and therefore had many more; which was a profitable thing to him, and a disadvantage to me. For, though I did indeed receive and send papers by the post, yet the public opinion was otherwise; for what I did send was by bribing the riders, who took them privately; Bradford being unkind enough to forbid it, which occasioned some resentment on my part; and I thought so meanly of the practice, that, when I afterwards came into his situation, I took care never to imitate it.

I had hitherto continued to board with Godfrey, who lived in a part of my house with his wife and children, and had one side of the shop for his glazier's business though he worked little, being always absorbed in his mathematics. Mrs. Godfrey projected a match for me, with a relation's daughter, took opportunities of bringing us often together, till a serious courtship on my part ensued; the girl being in herself very deserving. The old folks encouraged me by continual invitations to supper, and by leaving us together, till at length it was time to explain. Mrs. Godfrey managed our little treaty. I let her know that I expected as much money with their daughter as would pay off my remaining debt for the printing-house; which I believe was not then above a hundred pounds. She brought me word they had no such sum to spare; I said they might mortgage their house in the loan-office. The answer to this, after some days, was, that they did not approve the match; that, on inquiry of Bradford, they had been informed the printing business was not a profitable one, the types would soon be worn out and more wanted; that Keimer and David Harry had failed one after the other, and I should probably soon follow them; and therefore I was forbidden the house, and the daughter was shut up.

Whether this was a real change of sentiment or only artifice, on a supposition of our being too far engaged in ffaection to retract, and therefore that we should steal a marriage, which would leave them at liberty to give or withhold what they pleased, I know not. But I suspected the motive, resented it, and went no more. Mrs. Godfrey brought me afterwards some more favourable accounts of their disposition, and would have drawn me on again; but I declared absolutely my resolution to have nothing more to do with that family. This was resented by the Godfreys, we differed, and they removed, leaving me the whole house, and I resolved to take no more inmates.

But this affair having turned my thoughts to marriage, I looked round me and made overtures of acquaintance in other places; but soon found, that, the business of a printer being generally thought a poor one, I was not to expect money with a wife, unless with such a one as I should not otherwise think agreeable. In the mean time, that hard to be governed passion of youth had hurried me frequently into intrigues with low women that fell in my way, which were attended with some expense and great inconvenience, besides a continual risk to my health by a distemper, which of all things I dreaded, though by great good luck I escaped it.

A friendly correspondence as neighbours had continued between me and Miss Read's family, who all had a regard for me from the time of my first lodging in their house. I was often invited there and consulted in their affairs, wherein I sometimes was of service. I pitied poor Miss Read's unfortunate situation, who was generally dejected, seldom cheerful, and avoided company. I considered my giddiness and inconstancy when in London, as in a great degree the cause of her unhappiness; though the mother was good enough to think the fault more her own than mine, as she had prevented our marrying before I went thither, and persuaded the other match in my absence. Our mutual affection was revived, but there were now great objections to our union. That match was indeed looked upon as invalid, a preceding wife being said to be living in England; but this could not easily be proved, because of the distance, &c.; and, though there was a report of his death, it was not certain. Then, though it should be true, he had left many debts, which his successor might be called upon to pay. We ventured, however, over all these difficulties, and I took her to wife, September 1st, 1730. None of the inconveniences happened, that we had apprehended; she proved a good and faithful helpmate, assisted me much by attending to the shop; we throve together, and ever mutually endeavoured to make each other happy. Thus I corrected that great *erratum* as well as I could.

About this time, our club meeting, not at a tavern, but in a little room of Mr. Grace's, set apart for that purpose, a proposition was made by me, that, since our books were often referred to in our disquisitions upon the queries, it might be convenient

to us to have them all together where we met, that upon occasion
they might be consulted; and by thus clubbing our books in
a common library, we should, while we liked to keep them
together, have each of us the advantage of using the books of
all the other members, which would be nearly as beneficial as
if each owned the whole. It was liked and agreed to, and we
filled one end of the room with such books as we could best
spare. The number was not so great as we expected; and,
though they had been of great use, yet some inconveniences
occurring for want of due care of them, the collection after
about a year was separated; and each took his books home
again.

And now I set on foot my first project of a public nature—
that for a subscription library. I drew up the proposals, got
them put into form by our great scrivener, Brockden, and by
the help of my friends in the Junto, procured fifty subscribers
of forty shillings each to begin with, and ten shillings a year
for fifty years, the term our company was to continue. We
afterwards obtained a charter, the company being increased
to one hundred. This was the mother of all the North American subscription libraries, now so numerous; it is become a
great thing itself, and continually goes on increasing. These
libraries have improved the general conversation of the Americans, made the common tradesmen and farmers as intelligent
as most gentlemen from other countries, and perhaps have
contributed in some degree to the stand so generally made
throughout the colonies in defence of their privileges.

CHAPTER VI*.

At the time I established myself in Pennsylvania, there
was not a good bookseller's shop in any of the colonies to the
southward of Boston. In New York and Philadelphia, the
printers were indeed stationers; but they sold only paper,
almanacs, ballads, and a few common school-books. Those

* Down to this period the Memoir was written in the year 1771, and
the task was then laid aside for several years. In the mean time, the
manuscript was shown to several of the author's friends, who pressed him
to complete what he had begun. He accordingly yielded to their
solicitations, and, to the part with which this chapter commences, he prefixed the following introductory remarks, and also the two letters to
which he alludes.

who loved reading were obliged to send for their books from England; the members of the Junto had each a few. We had left the alehouse, where we first met, and hired a room to hold our club in. I proposed that we should all of us bring our books to that room, where they would not only be ready to consult in our conferences, but become a common benefit, each of us being at liberty to borrow such as he wished to read at home. This was accordingly done, and for some time contented us.

Finding the advantage of this little collection, I proposed to render the benefit from the books more common, by commencing a public subscription library. I drew a sketch of the plan and rules that would be necessary, and got a skilful conveyancer, Mr. Charles Brockden, to put the whole in form of articles of agreement to be subscribed; by which each subscriber engaged to pay a certain sum down for the first purchase of the books, and an annual contribution for increasing them. So few were the readers at that time in Philadelphia, and the majority of us so poor, that I was not able with great industry to find more than fifty persons, mostly young tradesmen, willing to pay down for this purpose forty shillings each, and ten shillings per annum. With this little fund we began. The books were imported. The library was opened one day in the week for lending them to subscribers, on their promissory notes to pay double the value if not duly returned. The institution soon manifested its

" *Continuation of the Account of my Life, begun at Passy, near Paris,* 1784.

" It is some time since I received the above letters, but I have been too busy till now to think of complying with the request they contain. It might, too, be much better done if I were at home among my papers, which would aid my memory, and help to ascertain dates; but my return being uncertain, and having just now a little leisure, I will endeavour to recollect and write what I can; if I live to get home, it may there be corrected and improved.

" Not having any copy here of what is already written, I know not whether any account is given of the means I used to establish the Philadelphia public library; which from a small beginning is now become so considerable. Though I remember to have come down to near the time of that transaction (1730). I will therefore begin here with an account of it, which may be struck out if found to have been already given."

The letters referred to were from his friends, Benjamin Vaughan and Abel James. They may be found in the *Correspondence*, Vol. IX. p. 478, under the date of January 31st, 1783.—ED.

utility, was imitated by other towns, and in other provinces. The libraries were augmented by donations, reading became fashionable; and our people having no public amusements to divert their attention from study, became better acquainted with books, and in a few years were observed by strangers to be better instructed and more intelligent than people of the same rank generally are in other countries.

When we were about to sign the abovementioned articles, which were to be binding on us, our heirs, &c. for fifty years, Mr. Brockden, the scrivener, said to us, " You are young men, but it is scarcely probable that any of you will live to see the expiration of the term fixed in the instrument." A number of us, however, are yet living; but the instrument was after a few years rendered null, by a charter that incorporated and gave perpetuity to the company.*

The objections and reluctances I met with in soliciting the

---

* It appears by a statement in Mr. Smith's " Notes for a History of the Library Company of Philadelphia," that the above " instrument " was dated July 1st. 1731. The charter of incorporation was obtained from the Proprietaries of Pennsylvania in 1742. Franklin's name stands at the head of the list of the persons who applied for the charter, and to whom it was granted. The library has grown to be one of the largest in America. The spacious and handsome edifice, in which it is contained, was erected but a short time before Dr. Franklin's death. It is stated in the minutes of the Library Company, as quoted by Mr. Smith, " that, upon the suggestion of Dr. Franklin, a large stone was prepared, and laid at the south-east corner of the building, with the following inscription, composed by the Doctor, except so far as relates to himself, which the Committee have taken the liberty of adding to it.

'Be it remembered,
In honour of the Philadelphia Youth,
(Then chiefly artificers,)
That in MDCCXXXI,
They cheerfully
At the Instance of Benjamin Franklin,
One of their Number,
Instituted the Philadelphia Library,
Which, though small at first,
Is become highly valuable, and extensively useful,
And which the Walls of this Edifice
Are now destined to contain and preserve ;
The first Stone of whose Foundation
Was here placed
The 31st of August, MDCCLXXXIX.' "

The marble statue of Dr. Franklin, which occupies a niche in front of the building, was executed in Italy, and presented to the Library Company by Mr. William Bingham. – ED.

subscriptions made me soon feel the impropriety of presenting
one's self as the proposer of any useful project that might be
supposed to raise one's reputation in the smallest degree
above that of one's neighbours, when one has need of their
assistance to accomplish that project. I therefore put myself
as much as I could out of sight, and stated it as a scheme of
a number of friends, who had requested me to go about and
propose it to such as they thought lovers of reading. In this
way my affair went on more smoothly, and I ever after practised it on such occasions; and, from my frequent successes,
can heartily recommend it. The present little sacrifice of
your vanity will afterwards be amply repaid. If it remains a
while uncertain to whom the merit belongs, some one more
vain than yourself may be encouraged to claim it, and then
even envy will be disposed to do you justice, by plucking
those assumed feathers, and restoring them to their right
owner.

This library afforded me the means of improvement by
constant study, for which I set apart an hour or two each day,
and thus repaired in some degree the loss of the learned
education my father once intended for me. Reading was the
only amusement I allowed myself. I spent no time in
taverns, games, or frolics of any kind; and my industry in
my business continued as indefatigable as it was necessary.
I was indebted for my printing-house; I had a young family
coming on to be educated, and I had two competitors to con-
tend with for business who were established in the place
before me. My circumstances, however, grew daily easier.
My original habits of frugality continuing, and my father
having, among his instructions to me when a boy, frequently
repeated a proverb of Solomon, "*Seest thou a man diligent in
his calling, he shall stand before kings, he shall not stand before
mean men*," I thence considered industry as a means of
obtaining wealth and distinction, which encouraged me,—
though I did not think that I should ever literally *stand before
kings*, which however has since happened; for I have stood
before *five*, and even had the honour of sitting down with one,
the King of Denmark, to dinner.

We have an English proverb that says, "*He that would
thrive must ask his wife.*" It was lucky for me that I had
one as much disposed to industry and frugality as myself.
She assisted me cheerfully in my business, folding and
stitching pamphlets, tending shop, purchasing old linen rags

for the paper-makers, &c. We kept no idle servants, our
table was plain and simple, our furniture of the cheapest.
For instance, my breakfast was for a long time bread and
milk (no tea), and I ate it out of a two-penny earthen porringer, with a pewter spoon. But mark how luxury will
enter families, and make a progress, in spite of principle;
being called one morning to breakfast, I found it in a china
bowl, with a spoon of silver! They had been bought for me
without my knowledge by my wife, and had cost her the
enormous sum of three and twenty shillings; for which she
had no other excuse or apology to make, but that she thought
her husband deserved a silver spoon and china bowl as well
as any of his neighbours. This was the first appearance of
plate and china in our house; which afterwards, in a course
of years, as our wealth increased, augmented gradually to
several hundred pounds in value.

I had been religiously educated as a Presbyterian; but,
though some of the dogmas of that persuasion, such as *the
eternal decrees of God, election, reprobation, &c.*, appeared to
me unintelligible, others doubtful, and I early absented
myself from the public assemblies of the sect, Sunday being
my studying day, I never was without some religious principles. I never doubted, for instance, the existence of a
Deity—that he made the world and governed it by his providence—that the most acceptable service of God was the doing
good to man—that our souls are immortal—and that all
crimes will be punished, and virtue rewarded, either here or
hereafter. These I esteemed the essentials of every religion;
and, being to be found in all the religions we had in our country,
I respected them all, though with different degrees of respect,
as I found them more or less mixed with other articles,
which, without any tendency to inspire, promote, or confirm
morality, served principally to divide us, and make us
unfriendly to one another. This respect to all, with an
opinion that the worst had some good effects, induced me to
avoid all discourse that might tend to lessen the good opinion
another might have of his own religion; and as our province
increased in people, and new places of worship were continually wanted, and generally erected by voluntary contribution, my mite for such purpose, whatever might be the
sect, was never refused.

Though I seldom attended any public worship, I had still
an opinion of its propriety, and of its utility, when rightly

conducted, and I regularly paid my annual subscription for
the support of the only Presbyterian minister or meeting we
had in Philadelphia.   He used to visit me sometimes as a
friend, and admonish me to attend his administrations; and I
was now and then prevailed on to do so ; once for five Sundays successively.   Had he been in my opinion a good
preacher, perhaps I might have continued, notwithstanding
the occasion I had for the Sunday's leisure in my course of
study; but his discourses were chiefly either polemic arguments, or explications of the peculiar doctrines of our sect,
and were all to me very dry, uninteresting, and unedifying;
since not a single moral principle was inculcated or enforced;
their aim seeming to be rather to make us *Presbyterians* than
good citizens.

At length he took for his text that verse of the fourth
chapter to the Philippians, "*Finally, brethren, whatsoever
things are true, honest, just, pure, lovely, or of good report, if
there be any virtue, or any praise, think on these things.*"   And
I imagined, in a sermon on such a text, we could not miss of
having some morality.   But he confined himself to five points
only, as meant by the apostle; 1. Keeping holy the Sabbath
day.   2. Being diligent in reading the holy Scriptures.   3.
Attending duly the public worship.   4. Partaking of the Sa-
crament.   5. Paying a due respect to God's ministers.   These
might be all good things; but, as they were not the kind of
good things that I expected from that text, I despaired of ever
meeting with them from any other, was disgusted, and attended
his preaching no more.   I had some years before composed a
little liturgy, or form of prayer, for my own private use, (in
1728,) entitled, *Articles of Belief and Acts of Religion*.   I returned to the use of this, and went no more to the public assemblies.   My conduct might be blamable, but I leave it,
without attempting further to excuse it; my present purpose
being to relate facts, and not to make apologies for them.*

---

* In Mr. Walsh's " Life of Franklin," published in Delaplaine's *Re-
pository*, there is an extract, copied from an original paper in Franklin's
handwriting, which claims insertion in this place, as connected with the
subject upon which the author is now about to speak.

" Those, who write of the art of poetry," says Franklin, "teach us,
that, if we would write what may be worth reading, we ought always,
before we begin, to form a regular plan and design of our piece ; otherwise we shall be in danger of incongruity.   I am apt to think it is the
same as to life.   I have never fixed a regular design in life, by which
means it has been a confused variety of different scenes.   I am now

It was about this time I conceived the bold and arduous project of arriving at *moral perfection*. I wished to live without committing any fault at any time, and to conquer all that either natural inclination, custom, or company, might lead me into. As I knew, or thought I knew, what was right and wrong, I did not see why I might not *always* do the one and avoid the other. But I soon found I had undertaken a task of more difficulty than I had imagined. While my attention was taken up, and care employed in guarding against one fault, I was often surprised by another; habit took the advantage of inattention; inclination was sometimes too strong for reason. I concluded at length, that the mere speculative conviction, that it was our interest to be completely virtuous, was not sufficient to prevent our slipping; and that the contrary habits must be broken, and good ones acquired and established, before we can have any dependence on a steady, uniform rectitude of conduct. For this purpose I therefore tried the following method.

In the various enumerations of the *moral virtues* I had met with in my reading, I found the catalogue more or less numerous, as different writers included more or fewer ideas under the same name. *Temperance*, for example, was by some confined to eating and drinking; while by others it was extended to mean the moderating every other pleasure, appetite, inclination, or passion, bodily or mental, even to our avarice and ambition. I proposed to myself, for the sake of clearness, to use rather more names, with fewer ideas annexed to each, than a few names with more ideas; and I included under thirteen

entering upon a new one; let me, therefore, make some resolutions, and form some scheme of action, that henceforth I may live in all respects like a rational creature.

"1. It is necessary for me to be extremely frugal for some time, till I have paid what I owe.

"2. To endeavour to speak truth in every instance, to give nobody expectations that are not likely to be answered, but aim at sincerity in every word and action; the most amiable excellence in a rational being.

"3. To apply myself industriously to whatever business I take in hand, and not divert my mind from my business by any foolish project of growing suddenly rich; for industry and patience are the surest means of plenty.

"4. I resolve to speak ill of no man whatever, not even in a matter of truth; but rather by some means excuse the faults I hear charged upon others, and, upon proper occasions, speak all the good I know of everybody."—ED.

names of virtues, all that at that time occurred to me as necessary or desirable; and annexed to each a short precept, which
fully expressed the extent I gave to its meaning.

These names of *virtues*, with their precepts, were;

1. TEMPERANCE.—Eat not to dulness; drink not to elevation.

2. SILENCE.—Speak not but what may benefit others or
yourself; avoid trifling conversation.

3. ORDER.—Let all your things have their places; let each
part of your business have its time.

4. RESOLUTION.—Resolve to perform what you ought;
perform without fail what you resolve.

5. FRUGALITY.—Make no expense but to do good to
others or yourself; that is, waste nothing.

6. INDUSTRY.—Lose no time; be always employed in
something useful; cut off all unnecessary actions.

7. SINCERITY.—Use no hurtful deceit; think innocently
and justly; and, if you speak, speak accordingly.

8. JUSTICE.—Wrong none by doing injuries, or omitting
the benefits that are your duty.

9. MODERATION.—Avoid extremes; forbear resenting injuries so much as you think they deserve.

10. CLEANLINESS.—Tolerate no uncleanliness in body,
clothes, or habitation.

11. TRANQUILLITY.—Be not disturbed at trifles, or at accidents common or unavoidable.

12. CHASTITY. . . . . .

13. HUMILITY.—Imitate Jesus and Socrates.

My intention being to acquire the *habitude* of all these virtues, I judged it would be well not to distract my attention by
attempting the whole at once, but to fix it on *one* of them at a
time; and, when I should be master of that, then to proceed
to another; and so on, till I should have gone through the
thirteen. And, as the previous acquisition of some might
facilitate the acquisition of certain others, I arranged them
with that view, as they stand above. *Temperance* first, as it
tends to procure that coolness and clearness of head, which is
so necessary, where constant vigilance was to be kept up, and
a guard maintained against the unremitting attraction of
ancient habits, and the force of perpetual temptations. This
being acquired and established, *Silence* would be more easy;
and my desire being to gain knowledge, at the same time that
I improved in virtue, and considering that in conversation it

was obtained rather by the use of the ear than of the tongue,
and therefore wishing to break a habit I was getting into of
prattling, punning, and jesting, which only made me acceptable to trifling company, I gave _Silence_ the second place.
This and the next, _Order_, I expected would allow me more
time for attending to my project and my studies. _Resolution_
once become habitual, would keep me firm in my endeavours
to obtain all the subsequent virtues; _Frugality_ and _Industry_
relieving me from my remaining debt, and producing affluence and independence, would make more easy the practice of
Sincerity and _Justice_, &c. &c. Conceiving then, that, agreeably to the advice of Pythagoras in his _Golden Verses_, daily
examination would be necessary, I contrived the following
method for conducting that examination.

I made a little book, in which I allotted a page for each of
the virtues. I ruled each page with red ink, so as to have
seven columns, one for each day of the week, marking each
column with a letter for the day. I crossed these columns
with thirteen red lines, marking the beginning of each line
with the first letter of one of the virtues; on which line, and
in its proper column, I might mark, by a little black spot,
every fault I found upon examination to have been committed
respecting that virtue, upon that day.*

I determined to give a week's strict attention to each of
the virtues successively. Thus, in the first week, my great

* This little book is dated _Sunday_, 1st July, 1733.--W. T. F.

In a letter written by the author to Lord Kames, in November, 1761,
he thus alludes to the scheme here mentioned, and to the design he
then had of expanding it into a treatise on the _Art of Virtue_. In that
letter he says; " To produce the number of valuable men necessary in a
nation for its prosperity, there is much more hope from schemes of _early
institution_ than from _reformation_. And, as the power of a single man
to do national service, in particular situations of influence, is often im-
mensely great, a writer can hardly conceive the good he may be doing,
when engaged in works of this kind. I cannot, therefore, but wish you
would publish it ["Elements of Criticism "] as soon as your other important employments will permit you to give it the finishing hand.
With these sentiments you will not doubt my being serious in the intention of finishing my _Art of Virtue._ It is not a mere ideal work. I
planned it first in 1732. I have from time to time made, and caused
to be made, experiments of the method with success. The materials
have been growing ever since. The form only is now to be given ; in
which I purpose employing my first leisure, after my return to my _other_
country." This project, as will be seen hereafter, was never carried into
effect.—ED.

FORM OF THE PAGES.

TEMPERANCE.

Eat not to dulness; drink not to elevation.

	Sun.	M.	T.	W.	Th.	F.	S.
Tem.							
Sil.	*	*		*		*	
Ord.	*	*			*	*	*
Res.		*				*	
Fru.		*				*	
Ind.			*				
Sinc.							
Jus.							
Mod.							
Clea.							
Tran.							
Chas.							
Hum.							

guard was to avoid every the least offence against *Temperance;* leaving the other virtues to their ordinary chance, only marking every evening the faults of the day. Thus, if in the first week I could keep my first line, marked T, clear of spots, I supposed the habit of that virtue so much strengthened, and its opposite weakened, that I might venture extending my attention to include the next, and for the following week keep both lines clear of spots. Proceeding thus to the last, I could get through a course complete in thirteen weeks, and four courses in a year. And like him, who, having a garden to weed, does not attempt to eradicate all the bad herbs at once, which would exceed his reach and his strength, but works on one of the beds at a time, and, having accomplished the first, proceeds to a second; so I should have, I hoped, the encouraging pleasure of seeing on my pages the progress made in virtue, by clearing successively my lines of their spots; till in the end, by a number of courses, I should be happy in viewing a clean book, after a thirteen weeks' daily examination.

This my little book had for its motto. these lines from Addison's *Cato ;*

> " Here will I hold.   If there 's a power above us,
> (And that there is, all nature cries aloud
> Through all her works,) He must delight in **virtue ;**
> And that which he delights in must be happy."

Another from Cicero,

" O vitæ Philosophia dux !   O virtutum indagatrix expultrixque vitiorum !   Unus dies, bene et ex præceptis tuis actus, peccanti immortalitati est anteponendus."

Another from the Proverbs of Solomon, speaking of wisdom or virtue ;

" Length of days is in her right hand, and in her left hand riches and honour.   Her ways are ways of pleasantness, and all her paths are peace."

And conceiving God to be the fountain of wisdom, I thought it right and necessary to solicit his assistance for obtaining it; to this end I formed the following little prayer, which was prefixed to my tables of examination, for daily use.

" O powerful Goodness ! bountiful father ! merciful Guide ! Increase in me that wisdom, which discovers my truest interest.   Strengthen my resolution to perform what that wisdom dictates.   Accept my kind offices to thy other children, as the only return in my power for thy continual favours to me."

I used also sometimes a little prayer which I took from Thomson's *Poems,* viz,

> "Father of light and life, thou Good Supreme !
> O teach me what is good ; teach me Thyself !
> Save me from folly, vanity, and vice,
> From every low pursuit ; and feed my soul
> With knowledge, conscious peace, and virtue pure ;
> Sacred, substantial, never-fading bliss !"

The precept of *Order* requiring that *every part of my business should have its allotted time,* one page in my little book contained the following scheme of employment for the twenty-four hours of a natural day.

I entered upon the execution of this plan for self-examination, and continued it with occasional intermissions for some time.   I was surprised to find myself so much fuller of faults than I had imagined ; but I had the satisfaction of seeing them diminish.   To avoid the trouble of renewing now and then my little book, which, by scraping out the marks on the paper of old faults to make room for new ones in a new

SCHEME.

Hours.

MORNING.
The *Question.* What good shall I do this day?

5	Rise, wash, and address *Power-*
6	*ful Goodness!* Contrive day's business, and take the resolution
7	of the day; prosecute the present study, and breakfast.

8	
9	
10	Work.
11	

NOON.

| 12 | Read, or look over my accounts, and dine. |
| 1 | |

AFTERNOON.

2	
3	. Work.
4	
5	

EVENING.
The *Question.* What good have I done to-day?

6	Put things in their places.
7	Supper. Music or diversion, or
8	conversation. Examination of
9	the day.

NIGHT.

10	
11	
12	
1	Sleep.
2	
3	
4	

course, became full of holes, I transferred my tables and precepts to the ivory leaves of a memorandum book, on which the lines were drawn with red ink, that made a durable stain; and on those lines I marked my faults with a black-lead pencil; which marks I could easily wipe out with a wet sponge. After awhile I went through one course only in a year; and afterwards only one in several years; till at length I omitted them entirely, being employed in voyages and business abroad with a multiplicity of affairs, that interfered; but I always carried my little book with me.

My scheme of *Order* gave me the most trouble: and I found, that, though it might be practicable where a man's business was such as to leave him the disposition of his time, that of a journeyman printer for instance, it was not possible to be exactly observed by a master, who must mix with the world, and often receive people of business at their own hours. Order, too, with regard to places for things, papers, &c., I found extremely difficult to acquire. I had not been early accustomed to *method*, and, having an exceedingly good memory, I was not so sensible of the inconvenience attending want of method. This article, therefore, cost me much painful attention, and my faults in it vexed me so much, and I made so little progress in amendment, and had such frequent relapses, that I was almost ready to give up the attempt, and content myself with a faulty character in that respect. Like the man, who, in buying an axe of a smith, my neighbour, desired to have the whole of its surface as bright as the edge. The smith consented to grind it bright for him, if he would turn the wheel; he turned, while the smith pressed the broad face of the axe hard and heavily on the stone, which made the turning of it very fatiguing. The man came every now and then from the wheel to see how the work went on; and at length would take his axe as it was, without further grinding. "No," said the smith, "turn on, turn on, we shall have it bright by and by; as yet it is only speckled." "Yes," said the man, "but *I think I like a speckled axe best.*" And I believe this may have been the case with many, who, having for want of some such means as I employed found the difficulty of obtaining good and breaking bad habits in other points of vice and virtue, have given up the struggle, and concluded that "*a speckled axe is best.*" For something, that pretended to be reason, was every now and then suggesting to me, that such extreme nicety as I exacted of myself might be a kind of foppery in morals, which, if it were known, would make me ridiculous; that a perfect character might be attended with the inconvenience of being envied and hated; and that a benevolent man should allow a few faults in himself, to keep his friends in countenance.

In truth, I found myself incorrigible with respect to *Order;* and now I am grown old, and my memory bad, I feel very sensibly the want of it. But on the whole, though I never arrived at the perfection I had been so ambitious of obtaining, but fell far short of it, yet I was, by the endeavour, a better and a happier man than I otherwise should have been, if I had not attempted it; as those who aim at perfect writing by imitating the engraved copies, though they never reach the wished-for excellence of those copies, their hand is mended by the endeavour, and is tolerable while it continues fair and legible.

It may be well my posterity should be informed, that to this little **artifice**, with the blessing of God, their ancestor owed the constant felicity of his life, down to his seventy-ninth year, in which this is written. What reverses may attend the remainder is in the hand of Providence; but, if they arrive, the reflection on past happiness enjoyed ought to help his bearing them with more resignation. To *Temperance* he ascribes his long continued health, and what is still left to him of a good constitution; to *Industry* and *Frugality*, the early easiness of his circumstances and acquisition of his fortune, with all that knowledge that enabled him to be a useful citizen, and obtained for him some degree of reputation among the learned; to *Sincerity* and *Justice*, the confidence of his country, and the honourable employs it conferred upon him; and to the joint influence of the whole mass of the virtues, even in the imperfect state he was able to acquire them, all that evenness of temper, and that cheerfulness in conversation, which makes his company still sought for, and agreeable even to his young acquaintance. I hope, therefore, that some of my descendants may follow the example and reap the benefit.

It will be remarked, that, though my scheme was not wholly without religion, there was in it no mark of any of the distinguishing tenets of any particular sect. I had purposely avoided them; for, being fully persuaded of the utility and excellency of my method, and that it might be serviceable to people in all religions, and intending some time or other to publish it, I would not have any thing in it that should prejudice any one, of any sect, against it. I proposed writing a little comment on each virtue, in which I would have shown the advantages of possessing it, and the mischiefs attending its opposite vice; I should have called my book THE ART OF VIRTUE, because it would have shown the means and manner of obtaining virtue, which would have distinguished it from the mere exhortation to be good, that does not instruct and indicate the means; but is like the Apostle's man of verbal charity, who, without showing to the naked and hungry, how or where they might get clothes or victuals, only exhorted them to be fed and clothed. *James* ii. 15, 16.

But it so happened, that my intention of writing and publishing this comment was never fulfilled. I had, indeed, from time to time, put down short hints of the sentiments and reasonings to be made use of in it; some of which I have still by me; but the necessary close attention to private business in the earlier part of life, and public business since, have occasioned my postponing it. For, it being connected in my mind with *a great and extensive project*, that required the whole man to execute, and which an unforeseen succession of employs prevented my attending to, it has hitherto remained unfinished.

In this piece it was my design to explain and enforce this doctrine, *that vicious actions are not hurtful because they are forbidden, but forbidden because they are hurtful*, the nature of man alone considered ; that it was, therefore, every one's interest to be virtuous, who wished to be happy even in this world ; and I should from this circumstance (there being always in the world a number of rich merchants, nobility, states, and princes, who have need of honest instruments for the management of their affairs, and such being so rare) have endeavoured to convince young persons, that no qualities are so likely to make a poor man's fortune, as those of *probity* and *integrity*.

My list of virtues contained at first but twelve ; but a Quaker friend having kindly informed me, that I was generally thought proud ; that my pride showed itself frequently in conversation ; that I was not content with being in the right when discussing any point, but was overbearing, and rather insolent, of which he convinced me by mentioning several instances ; I determined to endeavour to cure myself, if I could, of this vice or folly among the rest ; and I added *Humility* to my list, giving an extensive meaning to the word.

I cannot boast of much success in acquiring the *reality* of this virtue, but I had a good deal with regard to the appearance of it. I made it a rule to forbear all direct contradiction to the sentiments of others, and all positive assertion of my own. I even forbid myself, agreeably to the old laws of our Junto, the use of every word or expression in the language that imported a fixed opinion ; such as *certainly, undoubtedly*, &c., and I adopted instead of them, *I conceive, I apprehend*, or *I imagine*, a thing to be so or so ; or it so *appears to me at present*. When another asserted something that I thought an error, I denied myself the pleasure of contradicting him abruptly, and of showing immediately some absurdity in his proposition ; and in answering I began by observing, that, in certain cases or circumstances, his opinion would be right, but in the present case there *appeared* or *seemed to me* some difference, &c. I soon found the advantage of this change in **my manners** ; the conversations I engaged in went on more pleasantly. The modest way in which I proposed my opinions, procured them a readier reception and less contradiction; I had less mortification, when I was found to be in the wrong; and I more easily prevailed with others to give up their mistakes and join with me, when I happened to be in the right.

And this mode, which I at first put on with some violence to natural inclination, became at length easy, and so habitual to me, that perhaps for the last fifty years no one has ever heard a dogmatical expression escape me. And to this habit (after my character of integrity) I think it principally owing, that I had early so much weight with my fellow citizens, when I proposed new institutions or alterations in the old; and so much influence in public councils, when I became a member; for I was but a bad speaker, never eloquent, subject to much hesitation in my choice of words, hardly correct in language, and yet I generally carried my point.

In reality there is, perhaps, no one of our natural passions so hard to subdue as *pride*. Disguise it, struggle with it, stifle it, mortify it as much as one pleases, it is still alive, and will every now and then peep out and show itself; you will see it, perhaps, often in this history. For, even if I could conceive that I had completely overcome it, I should probably be *proud* of my *humility*.

CHAPTER VII.*

HAVING mentioned *a great and extensive project*, which I had conceived, it seems proper that some account should be here given of that project and its object. Its first rise in my mind appears in the following little paper, accidentally preserved, viz:

"*Observations on my reading history in the Library, May 9th*, 1731.

"That the great affairs of the world, the wars and revolutions, are carried on and effected by parties.

"That the view of these parties is their present general interest, or what they take to be such.

* The preceding chapter was written at Passy. In a memorandum which he made, when he again resumed the narrative four years afterwards, he says, "I am now about to write at home, (Philade'phia,) August, 1788, but cannot have the help expected from my papers, many of them being lost in the war. I have, however, found the following." He then proceeds as in the text.—ED.

" That the different views of these different parties occasion all confusion.

" That while a party is carrying on a general design, each man has his particular private interest in view.

" That as soon as a party has gained its general point, each member becomes intent upon his particular interest; which, thwarting others, breaks that party into divisions, and occasions more confusion.

" That few in public affairs act from a mere view of the good of their country, whatever they may pretend; and, though their actings bring real good to their country, yet men primarily considered that their own and their country's interest were united, and so did not act from a principle of benevolence.

" That fewer still in public affairs act with a view to the good of mankind.

" There seems to me at present to be great occasion for raising a *United Party for Virtue*, by forming the virtuous and good men of all nations into a regular body, to be governed by suitable good and wise rules, which good and wise men may probably be more unanimous in their obedience to than common people are to common laws.

" I at present think that whoever attempts this aright, and is well qualified, cannot fail of pleasing God and of meeting with success."

Revolving this project in my mind, as to be undertaken hereafter, when my circumstances should afford me the necessary leisure, I put down from time to time on pieces of paper, such thoughts as occurred to me respecting it. Most of these are lost; but I find one purporting to be the substance of an intended creed, containing, as I thought, the essentials of every known religion, and being free of every thing that might shock the professors of any religion. It is expressed in these words; viz.

" That there is one God, who made all things.

" That he governs the world by his providence.

" That he ought to be worshipped by adoration, prayer, and thanksgiving.

" But that the most acceptable service to God is doing good to man.

" That the soul is immortal.

" And that God will certainly reward virtue and punish vice, either here or hereafter."

My ideas at that time were, that the sect should be begun and spread at first among young and single men only; that each person to be initiated should not only declare his assent to such creed, but should have exercised himself with the thirteen weeks' examination and practice of the virtues, as in the beforementioned model; that the existence of such a society should be kept a secret, till it was become considerable, to prevent solicitations for the admission of improper persons; but that the members should, each of them, search among his acquaintance for ingenious, well-disposed youths, to whom, with prudent caution, the scheme should be gradually communicated. That the members should engage to afford their advice, assistance, and support to each other in promoting one another's interest, business, and advancement in life. That, for distinction, we should be called THE SOCIETY OF THE FREE AND EASY. Free, as being, by the general practice and habits of the virtues, free from the dominion of vice; and particularly, by the practice of industry and frugality. free from debt. which exposes a man to constraint, and a species of slavery to his creditors.

This is as much as I can now recollect of the project, except that I communicated it in part to two young men who adopted it with some enthusiasm; but my then narrow circumstances, and the necessity I was under of sticking close to my business, occasioned my postponing the further prosecution of it at that time; and my multifarious occupations, public and private, induced me to continue postponing, so that it has been omitted, till I have no longer strength or activity left sufficient for such an enterprise. Though I am still of opinion it was a practicable scheme, and might have been very useful, by forming a great number of good citizens; and I was not discouraged by the seeming magnitude of the undertaking, as I have always thought, that one man of tolerable abilities may work great changes, and accomplish great affairs among mankind, if he first forms a good plan; and, cutting off all amusements or other employments, that would divert his attention, makes the execution of that same plan his sole study and business.

In 1732, I first published my Almanac, under the name of *Richard Saunders;* it was continued by me about twenty-five years, and commonly called *Poor Richard's Almanac.** I

* Considering the remarkable success of this Almanac, and the great celebrity it has attained, particularly the summary of maxims selected from it and published separately under the title of *The Way to Wealth,* the reader may be curious to see the advertisement of the first number, including the table of contents. It was printed in the *Pennsylvania Gazette* on the 19th of December, 1732, as follows.

"Just published, for 1733, An Almanac, containing the Lunations, Eclipses, Planets' Motions and Aspects, Weather, Sun and Moon's Rising and Setting, High Water, &c.; besides many pleasant and witty Verses, Jests, and Sayings; Author's Motive of Writing; Prediction of the Death of his Friend, Mr. Titan Leeds; Moon no Cuckold; Bachelor's Folly; Parson's Wine and Baker's Pudding; Short Visits; Kings and Bears; New Fashions; Game for Kisses; Katherine's Love;

endeavoured to make it both entertaining and useful, and it accordingly came to be in such demand, that I reaped considerable profit from it; vending annually near ten thousand. And observing that it was generally read, scarce any neighbourhood in the province being without it, I considered it as a proper vehicle for conveying instruction among the common people, who bought scarcely any other books. I therefore filled all the little spaces, that occurred between the remarkable days in the Calendar, with proverbial sentences, chiefly such as inculcated industry and frugality, as the means of procuring wealth, and thereby securing virtue; it being more difficult for a man in want to act always honestly, as, to use here one of those proverbs, *it is hard for an empty sack to stand upright.*

These proverbs, which contained the wisdom of many ages and nations, I assembled and formed into a connected discourse prefixed to the Almanac of 1757, as the harangue of a wise old man to the people attending an auction. The bringing all these scattered counsels thus into a focus enabled them to make greater impression. The piece, being universally approved, was copied in all the newspapers of the American Continent, reprinted in Britain on a large sheet of paper,

Different Sentiments; Signs of a Tempest; Death of a Fisherman; Conjugal Debate; Men and Melons; The Prodigal; Breakfast in Bed; Oyster Lawsuit, &c. By Richard Saunders, Philomat. Printed and Sold by B. Franklin."

Such was the eagerness with which this Almanac was sought that three editions were printed before the end of January, and, although he enlarged his first editions for the subsequent years, yet two editions were frequently required to supply the demand. In the Almanac for 1739 he makes the following apology for its miscellaneous character.

"Besides the usual things expected in an Almanac, I hope the professed teachers of mankind will excuse my scattering here and there some instructive hints in matters of morality and religion. And be not thou disturbed, O grave and sober reader, if, among the many serious sentences in my book thou findest me trifling now and then and talking idly. In all the dishes I have hitherto cooked for thee there is solid meat enough for thy money. There are scraps from the table of wisdom that will, if well digested, yield strong nourishment for the mind. But squeamish stomachs cannot eat without pickles, which, it is true, are good for nothing else, but they provoke an appetite. The vain youth that reads my Almanac for the sake of an idle joke, will perhaps meet with a serious reflection that he may ever after be the better for."

It is believed that a complete series of *Poor Richard's Almanac* is not now in existence. After much research I have not been able to find more than one third of the numbers that were published.—Ed.

to be stuck up in houses; two translations were made of it in France, and great numbers bought by the clergy and gentry, to distribute gratis among their poor parishioners and tenants. In Pennsylvania, as it discouraged useless expense in foreign superfluities, some thought it had its share of influence in producing that growing plenty of money, which was observable for several years after its publication.

I considered my newspaper, also, as another means of communicating instruction, and in that view frequently reprinted in it extracts from the *Spectator*, and other moral writers; and sometimes published little pieces of my own, which had been first composed for reading in our Junto. Of these are a Socratic dialogue, tending to prove, that, whatever might be his parts and abilities, a vicious man could not properly be called a man of sense; and a discourse on self-denial, showing that virtue was not secure, till its practice became a *habitude*, and was free from the opposition of contrary inclinations. These may be found in the papers about the beginning of 1735.*

In the conduct of my newspaper, I carefully excluded all libelling and personal abuse, which is of late years become so disgraceful to our country. Whenever I was solicited to insert anything of that kind, and the writers pleaded, as they generally did, the liberty of the press; and that a newspaper was like a stage-coach, in which any one who would pay had a right to a place; my answer was, that I would print the piece separately if desired, and the author might have as many copies as he pleased to distribute himself; but that I would not take upon me to spread his detraction; and that, having contracted with my subscribers to furnish them with what might be either useful or entertaining, I could not fill their papers with private altercation, in which they had no concern, without doing them manifest injustice. Now, many of our printers make no scruple of gratifying the malice of individuals, by false accusations of the fairest characters among ourselves, augmenting animosity even to the producing of duels; and are, moreover, so indiscreet as to print scurrilous reflections on the government of neighbouring states, and even on the conduct of our best national allies, which may be attended with the most pernicious consequences. These things I mention as a caution to young printers, and that they

---

* The *Dialogue* was printed in the year 1730; and the other piece in 1735.—ED.

may be encouraged not to pollute their presses, and disgrace their profession by such infamous practices, but refuse steadily; as they may see by my example, that such a course of conduct will not on the whole be injurious to their interests.*

In 1733, I sent one of my journeymen to Charleston, South Carolina, where a printer was wanting. I furnished him with a press and letters, on an agreement of partnership, by which I was to receive one third of the profits of the business, paying one-third of the expense. He was a man of learning, but ignorant in matters of account; and, though he sometimes made me remittances, I could get no account from him, nor any satisfactory state of our partnership while he lived. On his decease, the business was continued by his widow, who, being born and bred in Holland, where, as I have been informed, the knowledge of accounts makes a part of female education, she not only sent me as clear a statement as she could find of the transactions past, but continued to account with the greatest regularity and exactness every quarter afterwards; and managed the business with such success, that she not only reputably brought up a family of children, but, at the expiration of the term, was able to purchase of me the printing-house, and establish her son in it.

I mention this affair chiefly for the sake of recommending that branch of education for our young women, as likely to be of more use to them and their children, in case of widowhood, than either music or dancing; by preserving them from losses by imposition of crafty men, and enabling them to continue, perhaps, a profitable mercantile house, with established correspondence, till a son is grown up fit to undertake and go on with it; to the lasting advantage and enriching of the family.

About the year 1734, there arrived among us a young Presbyterian preacher, named Hemphill, who delivered with a good voice, amd apparently extempore, most excellent discourses; which drew together considerable numbers of different persuasions, who joined in admiring them. Among the rest, I became one of his constant hearers, his sermons pleasing me, as they had little of the dogmatical kind, but inculcated strongly the practice of virtue, or what in the religious style are called *good works*. Those, however, of our

---

* In 1737 he published a piece in his paper on the Freedom of Speech and of the Press. Again, late in life, he wrote a pointed satirical piece on this subject.—ED.

congregation, who considered themselves as orthodox Presbyterians, disapproved his doctrine, and were joined by most of
the old ministers, who arraigned him of heterodoxy before
the synod, in order to have him silenced.   I became his zealous partisan, and contributed all I could to raise a party in
his favour, and combated for him awhile with some hopes of
success.   There was much scribbling *pro* and *con* upon the
occasion; and finding, that, though an elegant preacher, he
was but a poor writer, I wrote for him two or three pamphlets, and a piece in the *Gazette* of April, 1735.   Those pamphlets, as is generally the case with controversial writings,
though eagerly read at the time, were soon out of vogue, and
I question whether a single copy of them now exists.*

During the contest an unlucky occurrence hurt his cause
exceedingly.   One of our adversaries having heard him preach
a sermon, that was much admired, thought he had somewhere read the sermon before, or at least a part of it.   On
searching, he found that part quoted at length, in one of the
British *Reviews*, from a discourse of Dr. Foster's.   This
detection gave many of our party disgust, who accordingly
abandoned his cause, and occasioned our more speedy discom-
fiture in the synod.   I stuck by him, however; I rather approved his giving us good sermons composed by others, than
bad ones of his own manufacture; though the latter was the
practice of our common teachers.   He afterwards acknowledged to me, that none of those he preached were his own;
adding, that his memory was such, as enabled him to retain
and repeat any sermon after once reading only.   On our
defeat, he left us in search elsewhere of better fortune, and
I quitted the congregation, never attending it after; though
I continued many years my subscription for the support of its
ministers.

I had begun in 1733 to study languages; I soon made myself so much a master of the French, as to be able to read the
books in that language with ease.   I then undertook the Italian.   An acquaintance, who was also learning it, used often
to tempt me to play chess with him.   Finding this took up
too much of the time I had to spare for study, I at length

* None of these pamphlets has been found.   Several anonymous
tracts on this subject are advertised in the *Pennsylvania Gazette*, in the
months of July, September, and October, 1735, some of which are
probably the same that are here mentioned, as having been written by
Franklin.—Ed.

refused to play any more, unless on this condition, that the victor in every game should have a right to impose a task, either of parts of the grammar to be got by heart, or in translations, which tasks the vanquished was to perform upon honour before our next meeting.   As we played pretty equally, we thus beat one another into that language.   I afterwards, with a little pains-taking, acquired as much of the Spanish as to read their books also.

I have already mentioned that I had only one year's instruction in a Latin school, and that when very young, after which I neglected that language entirely.   But, when I had attained an acquaintance with the French, Italian, and Spanish, I was surprised to find, on looking over a Latin Testament, that I understood more of that language than I had imagined; which encouraged me to apply myself again to the study of it, and I met with more success, as those preceding languages had greatly smoothed my way.

From these circumstances I have thought there is some inconsistency in our common mode of teaching languages. We are told that it is proper to begin first with the Latin, and having acquired that, it will be more easy to attain those modern languages which are derived from it; and yet we do not begin with the Greek, in order more easily to acquire the Latin.   It is true that if we can clamber and get to the top of a staircase without using the steps, we shall more easily gain them in descending; but certainly if we begin with the lowest, we shall with more ease ascend to the top; and I would therefore offer it to the consideration of those who superintend the education of our youth, whether, since many of those, who begin with the Latin, quit the same after spending some years without having made any great proficiency, and what they have learned becomes almost useless, so that their time has been lost, it would not have been better to have begun with the French, proceeding to the Italian and Latin?   For though after spending the same time they should quit the study of languages and never arrive at the Latin, they would however have acquired another tongue or two, that, being in modern use, might be serviceable to them in common life.

After ten years' absence from Boston, and having become easy in my circumstances, I made a journey thither to visit my relations; which I could not sooner afford.   In returning I called at Newport to see my brother James, then settled there with his printing-house.   Our former differences were forgotten, and our meeting was very cordial and affectionate. He was fast declining in health, and requested me that, in case of his death, which he apprehended was not far distant, I would take home his son, then but ten years of age, and bring him up to the printing business. This I accordingly performed; sending him a few years to school before I took him into the office. His mother carried on the business till he was grown up, when I assisted him with an assortment of new types, those of his father being in a manner worn out. Thus it was that I made my brother ample amends for the service I had deprived him of by leaving him so early.

In 1736, I lost one of my sons, a fine boy of four years old, by the smallpox, taken in the common way. I long regretted him bitterly, and still regret that I had not given it to him by inoculation. This I mention for the sake of parents who omit that operation on the supposition that they should never forgive themselves if a child died under it; my example showing that the regret may be the same either way, and therefore that the safer should be chosen.

Our club, the Junto, was found so useful, and afforded such satisfaction to the members, that some were desirous of introducing their friends, which could not well be done without exceeding what we had settled as a convenient number, viz. twelve. We had from the beginning made it a rule to keep our institution a secret, which was pretty well observed; the intention was to avoid applications of improper persons for admittance, some of whom, perhaps, we might find it difficult to refuse. I was one of those who were against any addition to our number, but instead of it made in writing a proposal that every member separately should endeavour to form a subordinate club, with the same rules respecting queries, &c., and without informing them of the connexion with the Junto. The advantages proposed were the improvement of so many more young citizens by the use of our institutions; our better acquaintance with the general sentiments of the inhabitants on any occasion, as the Junto member might propose what queries we should desire, and was to report to the Junto what passed at his separate club; the promotion of our particular interests in business by more extensive recommendation, and the increase of our influence in public affairs, and our power of doing good by spreading through the several clubs the sentiments of the Junto.

The project was approved, and every member undertook to

form his club; but they did not all succeed. Five or six only were completed, which were called by different names, as the *Vine*, the *Union*, the *Band*. They were useful to themselves, and afforded us a good deal of amusement, information, and instruction; besides answering, in some considerable degree, our views of influencing the public on particular occasions; of which I shall give some instances in course of time as they happened.

My first promotion was my being chosen, in 1736, clerk of the General Assembly. The choice was made that year without opposition; but the year following, when I was again proposed, (the choice like that of the members being annual,) a new member made a long speech against me, in order to favour some other candidate. I was however chosen, which was the more agreeable to me, as, besides the pay for the immediate service of clerk, the place gave me a better opportunity of keeping up an interest among the members, which secured to me the business of printing the votes, laws, paper-money, and other occasional jobs for the public, that on the whole were very profitable.

I therefore did not like the opposition of this new member, who was a gentleman of fortune and education, with talents that were likely to give him in time great influence in the House, which indeed afterwards happened. I did not, however, aim at gaining his favour by paying any servile respect to him, but, after some time, took this other method. Having heard that he had in his library a certain very scarce and curious book, I wrote a note to him, expressing my desire of perusing that book, and requesting that he would do me the favour of lending it to me for a few days. He sent it immediately; and I returned it in about a week with another note, expressing strongly the sense of the favour. When we next met in the House he spoke to me, which he had never done before, and with great civility; and he ever after manifested a readiness to serve me on all occasions, so that we became great friends, and our friendship continued to his death. This is another instance of the truth of an old maxim I had learned, which says, "*He that has once done you a kindness will be more ready to do you another, than he whom you yourself have obliged.*" And it shows how much more profitable it is prudently to remove, than to resent, return, and continue, inimical proceedings.

In 1737, Colonel Spotswood, late governor of Virginia, and

then postmaster-general, being dissatisfied with the conduct of his deputy at Philadelphia, respecting some negligence in rendering, and want of exactness in framing, his accounts, took from him the commission and offered it to me. I accepted it readily, and found it of great advantage; for, though the salary was small, it facilitated the correspondence that improved my newspaper, increased the number demanded, as well as the advertisements to be inserted, so that it came to afford me a considerable income. My old competitor's newspaper declined proportionably, and I was satisfied without retaliating his refusal, while postmaster, to permit my papers being carried by the riders. Thus he suffered greatly from his neglect in due accounting; and I mention it as a lesson to those young men, who may be employed in managing affairs for others, that they should always render accounts, and make remittances, with great clearness and punctuality. The character of observing such a conduct is the most powerful of all recommendations to new employments and increase of business.*

* Before this appointment, he had been favoured in regard to the circulation of his newspaper. On the 28th of January, 1735, he says; " By the indulgence of the Honourable Colonel Spotswood, Post-master-General, the printer hereof is allowed to send the Gazettes by the post, postage free, to all parts of the post-road, from Virginia to New England."

The following advertisement indicates nearly the time at which he assumed the duties of postmaster, and also the degree of speed with which the mail was then conveyed.

October 27th, 1737.—" Notice is hereby given, that the post-office of Philadelphia is now kept at B. Franklin's, in Market Street; and that Henry Pratt is appointed Riding Postmaster for all the stages between Philadelphia and Newport in Virginia, who sets out about the beginning of each month, and returns in twenty-four days; by whom gentlemen, merchants, and others, may have their letters carefully conveyed, and business faithfully transacted, he having given good security for the same to the Honorable Colonel Spotswood, Postmaster-General of all his Majesty's dominions in America."

Six years afterwards some improvement had taken place in the transmission of the mail. In an advertisement dated April 14th, 1743, he says; " After this week the northern post will set out for New York on Thursdays at three o'clock in the forenoon till Christmas. The southern post sets out next Monday at eight o'clock for Annapolis, and continues going every fortnight during the summer season." In winter the post between Philadelphia and New York went once a fortnight.

The following characteristic advertisement is contained in the *Pennsylvania Gazette* for June 23rd, 1737.—" Taken out of a pew in the Church, some months since, a Common Prayer Book, bound in red, gilt,

I began now to turn my thoughts to public affairs, beginning, however, with small matters. The city watch was one of the first things that I conceived to want regulation. It was managed by the constables of the respective wards in turn; the constable summoned a number of housekeepers to attend him for the night. Those, who chose never to attend, paid him six shillings a year to be excused, which was supposed to go to hiring substitutes, but was in reality much more than was necessary for that purpose, and made the constableship a place of profit; and the constable, for a little drink, often got such ragamuffins about him as a watch, that respectable housekeepers did not choose to mix with. Walking the rounds, too, was often neglected, and most of the nights spent in tippling. I thereupon wrote a paper to be read in the Junto, representing these irregularities, but insisting more particularly on the inequality of the six shilling tax of the constable, respecting the circumstances of those who paid it; since a poor widow housekeeper, all whose property to be guarded by the watch did not perhaps exceed the value of fifty pounds, paid as much as the wealthiest merchant, who had thousands of pounds' worth of goods in his stores.

On the whole I proposed as a more effectual watch, the hiring of proper men to serve constantly in the business; and as a more equitable way of supporting the charge, the levying a tax that should be proportioned to the property. This idea, being approved by the Junto, was communicated to the other clubs, but as originating in each of them; and though the plan was not immediately carried into execution, yet, by preparing the minds of people for the change, it paved the way for the law obtained a few years after, when the members of our clubs were grown into more influence.

About this time I wrote a paper (first to be read in the Junto, but it was afterwards published,) on the different accidents and carelessnesses by which houses were set on fire, with cautions against them, and means proposed of avoiding them. This was spoken of as a useful piece, and gave rise to a project, which soon followed it, of forming a company for the more ready extinguishing of fires, and mutual assistance in removing and securing of goods when in danger.

and lettered D. F. [Deborah Franklin] on each cover. The person who took it is desired to open it and read the eighth Commandment and afterwards return it into the same pew again; upon which no further notice will be taken."—Ed.

Associates in this scheme were presently found amounting to thirty. Our articles of agreement obliged every member to keep always in good order, and fit for use, a certain number of leathern buckets, with strong bags and baskets (for packing and transporting of goods), which were to be brought to every fire; and we agreed about once a month to spend a social evening together, in discoursing and communicating such ideas as occurred to us upon the subject of fires, as might be useful in our conduct on such occasions.

The utility of this institution soon appeared, and many more desiring to be admitted than we thought convenient for one company, they were advised to form another, which was accordingly done; and thus went on one new company after another, till they became so numerous as to include most of the inhabitants who were men of property; and now, at the time of my writing this, though upwards of fifty years since its establishment, that which I first formed, called the *Union Fire Company*, still subsists; though the first members are all deceased but one, who is older by a year than I am. The fines that have been paid by members for absence at the monthly meetings have been applied to the purchase of fire-engines, ladders, fire-hooks, and other useful implements for each company; so that I question whether there is a city in the world better provided with the means of putting a stop to beginning conflagrations; and, in fact, since these institutions, the city has never lost by fire more than one or two houses at a time, and the flames have often been extinguished before the house in which they began has been half consumed

CHAPTER VIII.

In 1739, arrived among us from Ireland the Reverend Mr Whitefield, who had made himself remarkable there as an itinerant preacher. He was at first permitted to preach in some of our churches; but the clergy, taking a dislike to him, soon refused him their pulpits, and he was obliged to preach in the fields. The multitudes of all sects and denominations that attended his sermons were enormous, and it was a matter of speculation to me, who was one of the number, to observe the extraordinary influence of his oratory on his hearers, and how much they admired and respected him, notwithstanding his common abuse of them, by assuring them, they were naturally *half beasts and half devils.* It was wonderful to see the change soon made in the manners of our inhabitants. From being thoughtless or indifferent about religion, it seemed as if all the world were growing religious, so that one could not walk through the town in an evening without hearing psalms sung in different families of every street.

And it being found inconvenient to assemble in the open air, subject to its inclemencies, the building of a house to meet in was no sooner proposed, and persons appointed to receive contributions, than sufficient sums were soon received to procure the ground, and erect the building, which was one hundred feet long and seventy broad; and the work was carried on with such spirit as to be finished in a much shorter time than could have been expected. Both house and ground were vested in trustees, expressly for the use of *any preacher of any religious persuasion,* who might desire to say some thing to the people at Philadelphia; the design in building being not to accommodate any particular sect, but the inhabitants in general; so that even if the Mufti of Constantinople were to send a missionary to preach Mahometanism to us, he would find a pulpit at his service.

Mr. Whitefield, on leaving us, went preaching all the way through the colonies to Georgia. The settlement of that province had been lately begun, but, instead of being made with hardy, industrious husbandmen, accustomed to labour, the only people fit for such an enterprise, it was with families of broken shopkeepers and other insolvent debtors; many of indolent and idle habits, taken out of the jails, who, being set down in the woods, unqualified for clearing land, and unable to endure the hardships of a new settlement, perished in numbers, leaving many helpless children unprovided for. The sight of their miserable situation inspired the benevolent heart of Mr. Whitefield, with the idea of building an Orphan House there, in which they might be supported and educated. Returning northward, he preached up this charity, and made large collections; for his eloquence had a wonderful power over the hearts and purses of his hearers, of which I myself was an instance.

I did not disapprove of the design, but, as Georgia was then destitute of materials and workmen, and it was proposed to send them from Philadelphia at a great expense, I thought it would have been better to have built the house at Philadelphia.

H

and brought the children to it. This I advised; but he was resolute in his first project, rejected my counsel, and I therefore refused to contribute. I happened soon after to attend one of his sermons, in the course of which I perceived he intended to finish with a collection, and I silently resolved he should get nothing from me. I had in my pocket a handful of copper money, three or four silver dollars, and five pistoles in gold. As he proceeded I began to soften, and concluded to give the copper. Another stroke of his oratory made me ashamed of that, and determined me to give the silver; and he finished so admirably, that I emptied my pocket wholly into the collector's dish, gold and all. At this sermon there was also one of our club, who, being of my sentiments respecting the building in Georgia, and suspecting a collection might be intended, had by precaution emptied his pockets before he came from home. Towards the conclusion of the discourse, however, he felt a strong inclination to give, and applied to a neighbour, who stood near him, to lend him some money for the purpose. The request was fortunately made to perhaps the only man in the company, who had the firmness not to be affected by the preacher. His answer was, " At any other time, friend Hopkinson, I would lend to thee freely; but not now; for thee seems to be out of thy right senses."

Some of Mr. Whitefield's enemies affected to suppose that he would apply these collections to his own private emolument; but I, who was intimately acquainted with him, being employed in printing his Sermons and Journals, never had the least suspicion of his integrity; but am to this day decidedly of opinion, that he was in all his conduct a perfectly *honest man;* and methinks my testimony in his favour ought to have the more weight, as we had no religious connexion. He used, indeed, sometimes, to pray for my conversion, but never had the satisfaction of believing that his prayers were heard. Ours was a mere civil friendship, sincere on both sides, and lasted to his death.

The following instance will show the terms on which we stood. Upon one of his arrivals from England at Boston, he wrote to me, that he should come soon to Philadelphia, but knew not where he could lodge when there, as he understood his old friend and host, Mr. Benezet, was removed to Germantown. My answer was, " You know my house; if you can make shift with its scanty accommodations, you will be most heartily welcome." He replied, that if I made that kind offer for *Christ's* sake, I should not miss of a reward. And I returned, " Don't let me be mistaken; it was not for *Christ's* sake, but for *your* sake." One of our common acquaintance jocosely remarked, that, knowing it to be the custom of the saints, when they received any favour, to shift the burden of the obligation from off their own shoulders, and place it in heaven, I had contrived to fix it on earth.

The last time I saw Mr. Whitefield, was in London, when he consulted me about his Orphan-House concern, and his purpose of appropriating it to the establishment of a college.

He had a loud and clear voice, and articulated his words so perfectly, that he might be heard and understood at a great distance; especially as his auditors observed the most perfect silence. He preached one evening from the top of the Court-House steps, which are in the middle of Market Street, and on the west side of Second Street, which crosses it at right angles. Both streets were filled with his hearers to a considerable distance. Being among the hindmost in Market Street, I had the curiosity to learn how far he could be heard, by retiring backwards down the street towards the river; and I found his voice distinct till I came near Front Street, when some noise in that street obscured it. Imagining then a semicircle, of which my distance should be the radius, and that it was filled with auditors, to each of whom I allowed two square feet, I computed that he might well be heard by more than thirty thousand. This reconciled me to the newspaper accounts of his having preached to twenty-five thousand people in the fields, and to the history of generals haranguing whole armies, of which I had sometimes doubted.*

By hearing him often, I came to distinguish easily between sermons newly composed, and those which he had often preached in the course of his travels. His delivery of the

---

* In the early part of his life, Mr. Whitefield was preaching in an open field, when a drummer happened to be present, who was determined to interrupt his pious business, and rudely beat his drum in a violent manner, in order to drown the preacher's voice. Mr. Whitefield spoke very loud, but was not as powerful as the instrument. He therefore called out to the drummer in these words, " Friend, you and I serve the two greatest masters existing, but in different callings ; you beat up for volunteers for King George, I for the Lord Jesus. In God's name then let us not interrupt each other ; the world is wide enough for both; and we may get recruits in abundance." This speech had such an effect on the drummer that he went away in great good humour, and left the preacher in full possession of the field.

latter was so improved by frequent repetition, that every accent, every emphasis, every modulation of voice, was so perfectly well turned and well placed, that, without being interested in the subject, one could not help being pleased with the discourse; a pleasure of much the same kind with that received from an excellent piece of music. This is an advantage itinerant preachers have over those who are stationary, as the latter cannot well improve their delivery of a sermon by so many rehearsals.

His writing and printing from time to time gave great advantage to his enemies; unguarded expressions, and even erroneous opinions, delivered in preaching, might have been afterwards explained or qualified by supposing others that might have accompanied them; or they might have been denied; but *litera scripta manet*. Critics attacked his writings violently, and with so much appearance of reason as to diminish the number of his votaries, and prevent their increase. So that I am satisfied, that, if he had never written anything he would have left behind him a much more numerous and important sect; and his reputation might in that case have been still growing even after his death; as, there being nothing of his writing on which to found a censure, and give him a lower character, his proselytes would be left at liberty to attribute to him as great a variety of excellences, as their enthusiastic admiration might wish him to have possessed.*

* The following notices, selected from Franklin's newspaper, the *Pennsylvania Gazette*, show that he was the first publisher of Whitefield's writings ; and they also contain some curious facts respecting the success of that eloquent preacher, immediately after his arrival in America.

November 15th, 1739.—" The Reverend Mr. Whitefield, having given me copies of his Journals and Sermons, with leave to print the same, I propose to publish them with all expedition, if I find sufficient encouragement. The Sermons will make two volumes; and the Journals two more ; which will be delivered to subscribers at two shillings for each volume bound. Those, therefore, who are inclined to encourage this work, are desired speedily to send in their names to me, that I may take measures accordingly."

November 29th.—" On Friday last, Mr. Whitefield arrived here with his friends from New York, where he preached eight 'imes. He has preached twice every day to great crowds, except Tuesday, when he preached at Germantown, from a balcony, to about five thousand people in the street. And last night the crowd was so great to hear his farewell sermon, that the church could not contain one half, whereupon they withdrew to Society Hill, where he preached from a balcony to a multitude, computed at not less than ten thousand people. He left this city to-day."

My business was now constantly augmenting, and my circumstances growing daily easier, my newspaper having become very profitable, as being for a time almost the only one in this and the neighbouring provinces. I experienced too, the truth of the observation, "*that after getting the first hundred pounds, it is more easy to get the second;*" money itself being of a prolific nature.

The partnership at Carolina having succeeded, I was encouraged to engage in others, and to promote several of my workmen, who had behaved well, by establishing them in printing-houses in different colonies, on the same terms with that in Carolina.* Most of them did well, being enabled at the end

December 5th.—"On Thursday last, the Reverend Mr. Whitefield left this city, and was accompanied to Chester by about one hundred and fifty horse, and preached there to about seven thousand people. On Friday he preached twice at Willing's Town to about five thousand; on Saturday, at Newcastle, to about two thousand five hundred; and the same evening, at Christiana Bridge, to about three thousand; on Sunday, at White Clay Creek, he preached twice, resting about half an hour between the sermons, to about eight thousand, of whom three thousand it is computed came on horseback. It rained most of the time, and yet they stood in the open air."

May 15th, 1740.—"This evening the Reverend Mr. Whitefield went on board his sloop at Newcastle to sail for Georgia. On Sunday he preached twice at Philadelphia. The last was his farewell sermon, at which was a vast audience. On Monday he preached at Derby and Chester; on Tuesday, at Wilmington and White Clay Creek; on Wednesday, at Nottingham; on Thursday, at Fog's Manor. The congregations were, at every place, much more numerous than when he was here last. We hear that he has collected in these parts, in goods and money, between four and five hundred pounds sterling for his Orphan House in Georgia."

May 22d, 1740.—"Monday next will be delivered to the subscribers two volumes of the Reverend Mr. Whitefield's works; viz., one of Sermons, and one of Journals. The other volumes being nearly finished, will be ready in a short time. The whole number of names subscribed far exceeds the number of books printed. Those subscribers, who have paid, or who bring the money in their hands, will have the preference."—ED.

* By the general terms of these partnerships, Franklin supplied a printing-press and a certain quantity of types at his own charge; and all other materials for carrying on the business were provided by the partner. The amount of necessary expenses for rent, paper, ink, and the like, was deducted from the gross receipts, and the remainder, including the debts, was divided into three parts, of which two belonged to the partner and one to Franklin. All accounts were settled quarterly. At the expiration of the time agreed upon, which was commonly six years, the partner was at liberty to return the press and types, or to

of our term, six years, to purchase the types of me and go on
working for themselves, by which means several families were
raised.   Partnerships often finish in quarrels; but I was happy
in this, that mine were all carried on and ended amicably;
owing, I think, a good deal to the precaution of having very
explicitly settled, in our articles, every thing to be done by, or
expected from, each partner, so that there was nothing to dispute; which precaution I would therefore recommend to all
who enter into partnerships; for, whatever esteem partners
may have for, and confidence in, each other at the time of the
contract, little jealousies and disgusts may arise, with ideas of
inequality in the care and burden, business, &c., which are attended often with breach of friendship and of the connexion;
perhaps with lawsuits and other disagreeable consequences.

I had, on the whole, abundant reason to be satisfied with my
being established in Pennsylvania. There were, however,
some things that I regretted, there being no provision for
defence, nor for a complete education of youth; no militia,
nor any college. I, therefore, in 1743, drew up a proposal
for establishing an Academy; and at that time, thinking the
Reverend Richard Peters, who was out of employ, a fit person to superintend such an institution, I communicated the
project to him; but he, having more profitable views in the
service of the Proprietors, which succeeded, declined the
undertaking; and, not knowing another at that time suitable
for such a trust, I let the scheme lie awhile dormant. I succeeded better the next year, 1744, in proposing and establishing a *Philosophical Society*. The paper I wrote for that
purpose will be found among my writings, if not lost with
many others.

With respect to defence, Spain having been several years
at war against Great Britain, and being at length joined by
France, which brought us into great danger; and the laboured
and long-continued endeavour of our governor, Thomas, to
prevail with our Quaker Assembly to pass a militia law, and
make other provisions for the security of the province, having
proved abortive, I proposed to try what might be done by a
voluntary subscription of the people. To promote this, I
first wrote and published a pamphlet, entitled PLAIN TRUTH,
in which I stated our helpless situation in strong lights, with

purchase them at a fair valuation. A partnership of this description
existed for many years between Franklin and James Parker, a respectable printer in New York.—ED.

the necessity of union and discipline for our defence, and promised to propose in a few days an association, to be generally signed for that purpose. The pamphlet had a sudden and surprising effect. I was called upon for the instrument of association. Having settled the draft of it with a few friends, I appointed a meeting of the citizens in the large building before mentioned. The house was pretty full; I had prepared a number of printed copies, and provided pens and ink dispersed all over the room, I harangued them a little on the subject, read the paper, explained it, and then distributed the copies, which were eagerly signed, not the least objection being made.

When the company separated, and the papers were collected, we found above twelve hundred signatures; and other copies being dispersed in the country, the subscribers amounted at length to upwards of ten thousand. These all furnished themselves as soon as they could with arms, formed themselves into companies 'and regiments, chose their own officers, and met every week to be instructed in the manual exercise, and other parts of military discipline. The women, by subscriptions among themselves, provided silk colours, which they presented to the companies, painted with different devices and mottos, which I supplied. *

The officers of the companies composing the Philadelphia

* The following are the devices and mottos, as published at the time.

"1. A lion erect, a naked scimitar in one paw, the other holding the Pennsylvania scutcheon. Motto; *Patria.*

"2. Three arms, wearing different linen, ruffled, plain, and checked, the hands joined by grasping each other's wrist, denoting the union of all ranks. Motto; *Unita Virtus Valet.*

"3. An eagle, the emblem of Victory, descending from the skies. Motto; *A Deo Victoria.*

"4. The figure of Liberty sitting on a cube, holding a spear with the cap of Freedom on its point. Motto; *Inestimabilis.*

"5. An armed man with a naked falchion in his hand. Motto; *Deus adjuvat Fortes.*

"6. An elephant, being the emblem of a warrior always on his guard, as that creature is said never to lie down, and hath his arms ever in readiness. Motto; *Semper Paratus.*

"7. A city walled round. Motto; *Salus Patriæ Summa Lex.*

"8. A soldier with his piece recovered, ready to present. Motto; *Sic pacem quærimus.*

"9. A coronet and plume of feathers. Motto; *In God we trust.*

"10. A man with a sword drawn. Motto; *Pro Aris et Focis.*

"11. Three of the associators, marching with their muskets

regiment being met, cnose me for their colonel, but, con
ceiving myself unfit, I declined that station, and recommended Mr. Lawrence, a fine person, and a man of influence,
who was accordingly appointed. I then proposed a lottery
to defray the expense of building a battery below the town,
and furnished with cannon. It filled expeditiously, and the
battery was soon erected, the merlons being framed of logs,
and filled with earth.* We bought some old cannon from
Boston; but these not being sufficient we wrote to London

shouldered, and dressed in different clothes, intimating the unanimity
of the different sorts of people in the Association. Motto; *Vis Unita
Fortior.*

"12. A musket and sword crossing each other. Motto; *Pro Rege
et Grege.*

"13. Representation of a glory, in the middle of which is wrote,
JEHOVAH-NISSI; in English, *The Lord our Banner.*

"14. A castle, at the gate of which a soldier stands sentinel. Motto;
Cavendo Tutus.

"15. David, as he advanced against Goliath, and slung the stone.
Motto; *In Nomine Domini.*

"16. A lion rampant, one paw holding up a scimitar, another a sheaf
of wheat. Motto; *Domine Protege Alimentum.*

"17. A sleeping lion. Motto; *Rouse me if you dare.*

"18. Hope, represented by a woman standing clothed in blue,
holding one hand on an anchor. Motto; *Spero per deum Vincere.*

"19. Duke of Cumberland, as a general. Motto *Pro Deo et Georgio
Rege.*

"20. A soldier on horseback. Motto; *Pro Libertate Patriæ.*

"Most of the above colours, together with the officers' half-pikes and
spontoons, and even the halberts and drums, have been given by the
good ladies of this city, who raised money by subscription among themselves for that purpose."—*Pennsylvania Gazette, January 12th, and
April 14th,* 1748.—ED.

* It appears, that the Proprietaries were not pleased with this scheme
of associating for the defence of the province. They deemed it an
illegal act, and an exercise of too much power, to unite in this manner
without the previous sanction of the government; and they feared it
would prove a dangerous precedent, by encouraging the people to form
combinations for making new claims to civil privileges, and new en-
croachments on the prerogatives of the Proprietaries.

As cannon were afterwards sent from England, it is probable that the
Proprietaries became reconciled to the Association, when they were
more fully informed of its objects.

"The new large cannon, that lately arrived from England, purchased
by the managers of the lottery, being mounted on the great battery, on
Monday last, the associators of this city met under arms and marched
thither; where they were saluted with one and twenty guns, and named
the battery, THE ASSOCIATION."—*Pennsylvania Gazette, September 1st,*
1748.—ED.

for more, soliciting at the same time our Proprietaries
for some assistance, though without much expectation of
obtaining it.

Meanwhile Colonel Lawrence, Mr. Allen, Abraham Taylor,
and myself were sent to New York by the associators, commissioned to borrow some cannon of Governor Clinton.   He
at first refused us peremptorily; but at a dinner with his
council, where there was great drinking of Madeira wine, as
the custom of that place then was, he softened by degrees,
and said he would lend us six.   After a few more bumpers he
advanced to ten, and at length he very good-naturedly con-
ceded eighteen.   They were fine cannon, eighteen-pounders,
with their carriages, which were soon transported and mounted
on our batteries, where the associators kept a nightly guard,
while the war lasted, and among the rest I regularly took my
turn of duty there as a common soldier.

My activity in these operations was agreeable to the
Governor and Council; they took me into confidence, and I
was consulted by them in every measure where their concurrence was thought useful to the Association.   Calling in the
aid of religion, I proposed to them the proclaiming a fast, to
promote reformation, and implore the blessing of heaven on
our undertaking.   They embraced the motion; but, as it was
the first fast ever thought of in the province, the secretary
had no precedent from which to draw the proclamation.   My
education in New England, where a fast is proclaimed every
year, was here of some advantage; I drew it in the accustomed style; it was translated into German, printed in both
languages, and circulated through the province.   This gave
the clergy of the different sects an opportunity of influencing
their congregations to join the Association, and it would
probably have been general among all but the Quakers, if
the peace had not soon intervened.

It was thought by some of my friends, that, by my activity
in these affairs, I should offend that sect, and thereby lose
my interest in the Assembly of the province, where they
formed a great majority.   A young man, who had likewise
some friends in the Assembly, and wished to succeed me as
their clerk, acquainted me, that it was decided to displace
me at the next election; and he, through good will, advised
me to resign, as more consistent with my honour than being
turned out.   My answer to him was, that I had read or heard
of some public man, who made it a rule never to ask for an

office, and never to refuse one when offered to him. " I approve," said I, " of this rule, and shall practise it with a small addition; I shall never *ask*, never *refuse*, nor ever RESIGN an office. If they will have my office of clerk to dispose of it to another, they shall take it from me. I will not, by giving it up, lose my right of some time or other making reprisal on my adversaries." I heard, however, no more of this; I was chosen again unanimously as clerk at the next election. Possibly, as they disliked my late intimacy with the members of Council, who had joined the governors in all the disputes about military preparations, with which the House had long been harassed, they might have been pleased if I would voluntarily have left them; but they did not care to displace me on account merely of my zeal for the Association, and they could not well give another reason.

Indeed, I had some cause to believe that the defence of the country was not disagreeable to any of them, provided they were not required to assist in it. And I found that a much greater number of them than I could have imagined, though against *offensive* war, were clearly for the *defensive*. Many pamphlets *pro* and *con* were published on the subject, and some by good Quakers, in favour of *defence;* which, I believe, convinced most of their young people.

A transaction in our fire company gave me some insight into their prevailing sentiments. It had been proposed that we should encourage the scheme for building a battery by laying out the present stock, then about sixty pounds, in tickets of the lottery. By our rules no money could be disposed of till the next meeting after the proposal. The company consisted of thirty members, of whom twenty-two were Quakers, and eight only of other persuasions. We eight punctually attended the meeting, but, though we thought that some of the Quakers would join us, we were by no means sure of a majority. Only one Quaker, Mr. James Morris, appeared to oppose the measure. He expressed much sorrow that it had ever been proposed, as he said *Friends* were all against it, and it would create such discord as might break up the company. We told him that we saw no reason for that ; we were the minority, and if *Friends* were against the measure and out-voted us we must and should, agreeably to the usage of all societies, submit. When the hour for business arrived, it was moved to put this to the vote ; he allowed we might do it by the rules, but, as he could assure us that a number of members intended to be present for the purpose of opposing it, it would be but candid to allow a little time for their appearing.

While we were disputing this a waiter came to tell me that two gentlemen below desired to speak with me. I went down, and found there two of our Quaker members. They told me there were eight of them assembled at a tavern just by; that they were determined to come and vote with us if there should be occasion, which they hoped would not be the case, and desired we would not call for their assistance if we could do without it, as their voting for such a measure might embroil them with their elders and friends. Being thus secure of a majority I went up, and, after a little seeming hesitation, agreed to a delay of another hour. This Mr. Morris allowed to be extremely fair. Not one of his opposing friends appeared, at which he expressed great surprise; and, at the expiration of the hour, we carried the resolution eight to one; and as of the twenty-two Quakers eight were ready to vote with us, and thirteen by their absence manifested that they were not inclined to oppose the measure, I afterwards estimated the proportion of Quakers sincerely against defence as one to twenty-one only. For these were all regular members of the society and in good reputation among them, and who had notice of what was proposed at that meeting.

The honourable and learned Mr. Logan, who had always been of that sect, wrote an address to them, declaring his approbation of *defensive* war, and supported his opinion by many strong arguments. He put into my hands sixty pounds to be laid out in lottery tickets for the battery, with directions to apply what prizes might be drawn wholly to that service He told me the following anecdote of his old master, William Penn, respecting defence. He came over from England when a young man with that Proprietary, and as his secretary. It was war time, and their ship was chased by an armed vessel, supposed to be an enemy. Their captain prepared for defence, but told William Penn and his company of Quakers that he did not expect their assistance, and they might retire into the cabin, which they did, except James Logan, who chose to stay upon deck, and was quartered to a gun. The supposed enemy proved a friend, so there was no fighting; but when the secretary went down to communicate the intelligence, William Penn rebuked him severely for staying upon deck, and undertaking to assist in defending the vessel, contrary to the principles of Friends; especially as it had not been required by the captain. This reprimand, being before all the company, piqued the secretary, who answered, " I being thy servant, why did thee not order me to come down? But thee was willing enough that I should stay and help to fight the ship when thee thought there was danger."

My being many years in the Assembly, a majority of which were constantly Quakers, gave me frequent opportunities of seeing the embarrassment given them by their principle against war whenever application was made to them, by order of the crown, to grant aids for military purposes. They were unwilling to offend government, on the one hand, by a direct refusal, and their friends, the body of the Quakers, on the other by a compliance contrary to their principles, using a variety of evasions to avoid complying, and modes of disguising the compliance when it became unavoidable. The common mode at last was to grant money under the phrase of its being "*for the King's use*," and never to inquire how it was applied.

But if the demand was not directly from the crown, that phrase was found not so proper, and some other was to be invented. Thus, when powder was wanting (I think it was for the garrison at Louisburg) and the government of New England solicited a grant of some from Pennsylvania, which was much urged on the House by Governor Thomas, they would not grant money to buy *powder*, because that was an ingredient of war, but they voted an aid to New England of three thousand pounds, to be put into the hands of the Governor, and appropriated it for the purchase of bread, flour, wheat, or *other grain*. Some of the Council, desirous of giving the House still further embarrassment, advised the Governor not to accept that provision, as not being the thing he had demanded; but he replied, " I shall take the money, for I understand very well their meaning; *other grain* is gunpowder;" which he accordingly bought, and they never objected to it.

It was in allusion to this fact, that when in our fire company we feared the success of our proposal in favour of the lottery, and I had said to a friend of mine, one of our members, " If we fail, let us move the purchase of a fire engine with the money, the Quakers can have no objection to that: and then, if you nominate me and I you as a committee for that purpose, we will buy a great gun, which is certainly a *fire engine*:" " I see," said he, " you have improved by being so long in the

Assembly; your equivocal project would be just a match for their wheat or *other grain*."

Those embarrassments that the Quakers suffered, from having established and published it as one of their principles that no kind of war was lawful, and which, being once published, they could not afterwards, however they might change their minds, easily get rid of, reminds me of what I think a more prudent conduct in another sect among us, that of the Dunkers. I was acquainted with one of its founders, Michael Weffare, soon after it appeared. He complained to me that they were grievously calumniated by the zealots of other persuasions, and charged with abominable principles and practices to which they were utter strangers. I told him this had always been the case with new sects, and that to put a stop to such abuse I imagined it might be well to publish the articles of their belief and the rules of their discipline. He said that it had been proposed among them, but not agreed to for this reason: " When we were first drawn together as a society," said he, " it had pleased God to enlighten our minds so far as to see that some doctrines which were esteemed truths were errors, and that others which we had esteemed errors were real truths. From time to time He has been pleased to afford us further light, and our principles have been improving and our errors diminishing. Now we are not sure that we are arrived at the end of this progression and at the perfection of spiritual or theological knowledge; and we fear that if we should once print our confession of faith, we should feel ourselves as if bound and confined by it, and perhaps be unwilling to receive further improvement, and our successors still more so, as conceiving what their elders and founders had done to be something sacred—never to be departed from."

This modesty in a sect is perhaps a single instance in the history of mankind, every other sect supposing itself in possession of all truth, and that those who differ are so far in the wrong; like a man travelling in foggy weather, those at some distance before him on the road he sees wrapped up in the fog as well as those behind him, and also the people in the fields on each side; but near him all appears clear, though, in truth, he is as much in the fog as any of them. To avoid this kind of embarrassment the Quakers have of late years been gradually declining the public service in the Assembly and in the magistracy, choosing rather to quit their power than their principle.

In order of time I should have mentioned before that
having, in 1742, invented an open stove for the better warming
of rooms, and at the same time saving fuel, as the fresh air
was warmed in entering, I made a present of the model to Mr.
Robert Grace, one of my early friends, who, having an iron
furnace, found the casting of the plates for these stoves a
profitable thing, as they were growing in demand.   To
promote that demand I wrote and published a pamphlet
entitled "An Account of the new-invented Pennsylvanian
Fire-places, wherein their Construction and Manner of Operation are particularly explained, their advantages above every
other Method of Warming Rooms demonstrated, and all
Objections that have been raised against the Use of them
answered and obviated," &c.   This pamphlet had a good
effect; Governor Thomas was so pleased with the construction
of this stove, as described in it, that he offered to give me a
patent for the sole vending of them for a term of years, but I
declined it from a principle which has ever weighed with me
on such occasions, viz., *that as we enjoy great advantages
from the inventions of others, we should be glad of an opportunity to serve others by any invention of ours, and this we
should do freely and generously.*

An ironmonger in London, however, assuming a good deal
of my pamphlet, and working it up into his own, and making
some small changes in the machine, which rather hurt its
operation, got a patent for it there, and made, as I was told, a
little fortune by it.   And this is not the only instance of patents taken out of my inventions by others, though not always
with the same success; which I never contested, as having no
desire of profiting by patents myself, and hating disputes.
The use of these fire-places in very many houses, both here in
Pennsylvania, and the neighbouring States, has been, and is,
a great saving of wood to the inhabitants.

CHAPTER IX.

PEACE being concluded, and the Association business
therefore at an end, I turned my thoughts again to the affair
of establishing an academy.   The first step I took was to as-
sociate in the design a number of active friends, of whom the
Junto furnished a good part; the next was to write and pub-

lish a pamphlet, entitled, *Proposals relating to the Education of Youth in Pennsylvania.* This I distributed among the principal inhabitants gratis; and as soon as I could suppose their minds a little prepared by the perusal of it, I set on foot a subscription for opening and supporting an academy; it was to be paid in quotas yearly for five years; by so dividing it I judged the subscription might be larger; and I believe it was so, amounting to no less, if I remember right, than five thousand pounds.

In the introduction to these proposals, I stated their publication not as an act of mine, but of some *public spirited gentlemen;* avoiding as much as I could, according to my usual rule, the presenting myself to the public as the author of any scheme for their benefit.

The subscribers, to carry the project into immediate execution, chose out of their number twenty-four trustees, and appointed Mr. Francis, then attorney-general, and myself, to draw up constitutions for the government of the academy; which being done and signed, a house was hired, masters engaged, and the schools opened; I think in the same year, 1749.

The scholars increasing fast, the house was soon found too small, and we were looking out for a piece of ground, properly situated, with intent to build, when accident threw into our way a large house ready built, which with a few alterations might well serve our purpose. This was the building before mentioned, erected by the hearers of Mr. Whitefield, and was obtained for us in the following manner.

It is to be noted, that, the contributions to this building being made by people of different sects, care was taken in the nomination of trustees, in whom the building and ground were to be vested, that a predominancy should not be given to any sect, lest in time that predominancy might be a means of appropriating the whole to the use of such sect, contrary to the original intention. It was for this reason, that one of each sect was appointed: viz., one Church-of-England man, one Presbyterian, one Baptist, one Moravian, &c., who, in case of vacancy by death, were to fill it by election from among the contributors. The Moravian happened not to please his colleagues, and on his death they resolved to have no other of that sect. The difficulty then was, how to avoid having two of some other sect, by means of the new choice.

Several persons were named, and for that reason not agreed

to. At length one mentioned me, with the observation, that I was merely an honest man, and of *no sect* at all, which prevailed with them to choose me. The enthusiasm, which existed when the house was built, had long since abated, and its trustees had not been able to procure fresh contributions for paying the ground rent, and discharging some other debts the building had occasioned, which embarrassed them greatly. Being now a member of both boards of trustees, that for the building, and that for the academy, I had a good opportunity of negotiating with both, and brought them finally to an agreement, by which the trustees for the building were to cede it to those of the academy; the latter undertaking to discharge the debt, to keep for ever open in the building a large hall for occasional preachers, according to the original intention, and maintain a free school for the instruction of poor children. Writings were accordingly drawn: and, on paying the debts, the trustees of the academy were put in possession of the premises; and, by dividing the great and lofty hall into stories, and different rooms above and below for the several schools, and purchasing some additional ground, the whole was soon made fit for our purpose, and the scholars removed into the building. The whole care and trouble of agreeing with the workmen, purchasing materials, and superintending the work, fell upon me; and I went through it the more cheerfully, as it did not then interfere with my private business; having the year before taken a very able, industrious, and honest partner, Mr. David Hall, with whose character I was well acquainted, as he had worked for me four years. He took off my hands all care of the printing-office, paying me punctually my share of the profits. This partnership continued eighteen years, successfully for us both.

The trustees of the academy, after a while, were incorporated by a charter from the governor; their funds were increased by contributions in Britain, and grants of land from the Proprietaries, to which the Assembly has since made considerable addition; and thus was established the present University of Philadelphia. I have been continued one of its trustees from the beginning, now near forty years, and have had the very great pleasure of seeing a number of the youth, who have received their education in it, distinguished by their improved abilities, serviceable in public stations, and ornaments to their country.*

* A free school was likewise attached to the academy, as appears by

When I was disengaged myself, as above mentioned, from private business, I flattered myself that, by the sufficient though moderate fortune I had acquired, I had found leisure during the rest of my life for philosophical studies and amusements.   I purchased all Dr. Spence's apparatus, who had come from England to lecture in Philadelphia, and I proceeded in my electrical experiments with great alacrity; but the public, now considering me as a man of leisure, laid hold of me for their purposes; every part of our civil government, and almost at the same time, imposing some duty upon me. The Governor put me into the commission of the peace; the corporation of the city chose me one of the common council, and soon after alderman; and the citizens at large elected me a burgess to represent them in the Assembly.   This latter station was the more agreeable to me, as I grew at length tired with sitting there to hear the debates, in which, as clerk, I could take no part; and which were often so uninteresting, that I was induced to amuse myself with making magic squares or circles, or any thing to avoid weariness; and I conceived my becoming a member would enlarge my power of doing good.   I would not however insinuate, that my ambition was not flattered by all these promotions; it certainly was, for, considering my low beginning, they were great things to me; and they were still more pleasing, as being so many spontaneous testimonies of the public good opinion, and by me entirely unsolicited.

The office of justice of the peace I tried a little, by attending a few courts, and sitting on the bench to hear causes; but finding that more knowledge of the common law than I possessed was necessary to act in that station with credit, I gradually withdrew from it; excusing myself by being obliged to the following advertisement in Franklin's *Gazette*, of September 19th, 1751.

" Notice is hereby given, that on Monday, the 16th of this instant September, a *free school* will be opened, under the care and direction of the Trustees of the Academy, at the New Building, for the instruction of poor children *gratis* in reading, writing, and arithmetic. Those who are desirous of having their children admitted, may apply to any of the Trustees."

Again, October 26th, 1752. " The charity school, opened by the Trustees in the Academy, now teaches reading, writing, and arithmetic to a hundred poor children, most of whom, though from eight to thirteen years of age, had never been sent to any school before; nor did it seem likely many of them would ever have been sent to any school, if it had not been for this institution."- -ED.

r

attend the higher duties of a legislator in the Assembly. My election to this trust was repeated every year for ten years, without my ever asking any elector for his vote, or signifying, either directly or indirectly, any desire of being chosen. On taking my seat in the House, my son was appointed their clerk.

The year following, a treaty being to be held with the Indians at Carlisle, the Governor sent a message to the House, proposing that they should nominate some of their members, to be joined with some members of Council, as commissioners for that purpose. The House named the Speaker (Mr. Norris) and myself; and, being commissioned, we went to Carlisle, and met the Indians accordingly.

As those people are extremely apt to get drunk, and when so are very quarrelsome and disorderly, we strictly forbade the selling any liquor to them; and when they complained of this restriction, we told them that if they would continue sober during the treaty, we would give them plenty of rum when the business was over. They promised this, and they kept their promise, because they could get no rum; and the treaty was conducted very orderly, and concluded to mutual satisfaction. They then claimed and received the rum; this was in the afternoon. They were near one hundred men, women, and children; and were lodged in temporary cabins, built in the form of a square, just without the town. In the evening, hearing a great noise among them, the commissioners walked to see what was the matter. We found they had made a great bonfire in the middle of the square; they were all drunk, men and women, quarrelling and fighting. Their dark-coloured bodies, half naked, seen only by the gloomy light of the bonfire, running after and beating one another with firebrands, accompanied by their horrid yellings, formed a scene the most resembling our ideas of hell that could well be imagined. There was no appeasing the tumult, and we retired to our lodging. At midnight a number of them came thundering at our door, demanding more rum, of which we took no notice.

The next day, sensible they had misbehaved in giving us that disturbance, they sent three of their old counsellors to make their apology. The orator acknowledged the fault, but laid it upon the rum; and then endeavoured to excuse the rum, by saying, " The Great Spirit, who made all things, made everything for some use; and whatever use he designed anything for, that use it should always be put to. Now, when he made rum, he said, ' *Let this be for the Indians to get drunk with;*' and it must be so." And, indeed, if it be the design of Providence to extirpate these savages in order to make room for the cultivators of the earth, it seems not impossible that rum may be the appointed means. It has already annihilated all the tribes who formerly inhabited the sea-coast.

In 1751, Dr. Thomas Bond, a particular friend of mine, conceived the idea of establishing a hospital in Philadelphia, (a very beneficent design, which has been ascribed to me, but was originally and truly his,) for the reception and cure of poor sick persons, whether inhabitants of the province or strangers. He was zealous and active in endeavouring to procure subscriptions for it; but the proposal being a novelty in America, and at first not well understood, he met but with little success.

At length he came to me with the compliment, that he found there was no such a thing as carrying a public-spirited project through without my being concerned in it. "For," said he, "I am often asked by those to whom I propose subscribing, *Have you consulted Franklin on this business? And what does he think of it?* And when I tell them that I have not, supposing it rather out of your line, they do not subscribe, but say, *they will consider it.*" I inquired into the nature and probable utility of this scheme, and receiving from him a very satisfactory explanation, I not only subscribed to it myself, but engaged heartily in the design of procuring subscriptions from others. Previously, however, to the solicitation, I endeavoured to prepare the minds of the people by writing on the subject in the newspapers, which was my usual custom in such cases, but which Dr. Bond had omitted.

The subscriptions afterwards were more free and generous : but, beginning to flag, I saw they would be insufficient without some assistance from the Assembly, and therefore proposed to petition for it, which was done. The country members did not at first relish the project. They objected that it could only be serviceable to the city, and therefore the citizens alone should be at the expense of it; and they doubted whether the citizens themselves generally approved of it. My allegation on the contrary, that it met with such approbation as to leave no doubt of our being able to raise two thousand pounds by voluntary donations, they considered as a most extravagant supposition, and utterly impossible.

I 2

On this I formed my plan ; and, asking leave to bring in a Bill for incorporating the contributors according to the prayer of their petition, and granting them a blank sum of money ; which leave was obtained chiefly on the consideration that the House could throw the Bill out if they did not like it. I drew it so as to make the important clause a conditional one : viz. " And be it enacted, by the authority aforesaid, that, when the said contributors shall have met and chosen their managers and treasurer, and shall have raised by their contributions a capital stock of two thousand pounds' value. (the yearly interest of which is to be applied to the accommodation of the sick poor in the said hospital, and of charge for diet, attendance, advice, and medicines,) and *shall make the same appear to the satisfaction of the Speaker of the Assembly for the time being*, that then it shall and may be lawful for the said Speaker, and he is hereby required, to sign an order on the provincial treasurer, for the payment of two thousand pounds, in two yearly payments, to the treasurer of the said hospital, to be applied to the founding, building, and finishing of the same."

This condition carried the Bill through ; for the members who had opposed the grant, and now conceived they might have the credit of being charitable without the expense, agreed to its passage. And then, in soliciting subscriptions among the people, we urged the conditional promise of the law as an additional motive to give, since every man's donation would be doubled ; thus the clause worked both ways. The subscriptions accordingly soon exceeded the requisite sum, and we claimed and received the public gift, which enabled us to carry the design into execution. A convenient and handsome building was soon erected ; the institution has by constant experience been found useful, and flourishes to this day ; and I do not remember any of my political manœuvres the success of which at the time gave me more pleasure, or wherein, after thinking of it, I more easily excused myself for having made some use of cunning.*

* The principal facts, respecting the origin and establishment of the Hospital, are contained in a quarto pamphlet, entitled " *Some Account of the Pennsylvania Hospital from its first Rise to the Beginning of the Fifth Month, called May,* 1754. *Philadelphia ; printed by B. Franklin and D. Hall.*" The *Bill,* alluded to in the text, makes a part of this pamphlet ; and also two papers previously published in the *Pennsylvania Gazette,* showing the benefits of such an institution, and urging contributions to the fund from motives of benevolence and

It was about this time that another projector, the Reve-rend Gilbert Tennent, came to me with a request, that I would assist him in procuring a subscription for erecting a new meeting-house.   It was to be for the use of a congre-gation he had gathered among the Presbyterians, who were originally disciples of Mr. Whitefield.   Unwilling to make myself disagreeable to my fellow citizens, by too frequently soliciting their contributions, I absolutely refused.   He then desired I would furnish him with a list of the names of per-sons I knew by experience to be generous and public-spirited. I thought it would be unbecoming in me, after their kind compliance with my solicitations, to mark them out to be worried by other beggars, and therefore refused to give such a list.   He then desired I would at least give him my advice. " That I will readily do," said I ; " and, in the first place, I advise you to apply to all those, who you know will give something ; next to those who you are uncertain whether they will give anything or not, and show them the list of those who have given ; and lastly, do not neglect those who you are sure will give nothing ; for in some of them you may be mistaken."   He laughed and thanked me, and said he would take my advice,   He did so, for he asked of *everybody;* and he obtained a much larger sum than he expected, with which he erected the capacious and elegant meeting-house that stands in Arch Street.

Our city, though laid out with a beautiful regularity, the streets large, straight, and crossing each other at right angles, had the disgrace of suffering those streets to remain long unpaved, and in wet weather the wheels of heavy carriages ploughed them into a quagmire, so that it was difficult to cross them ; and in dry weather the dust was offensive.   I had lived near what was called the Jersey Market, and saw with pain the inhabitants wading in mud, while purchasing their provisions.   A strip of ground down the middle of that market was at length paved with brick, so that, being once in the market, they had firm footing ; but were often over shoes in dirt to get there.   By talking and writing on the subject, I was at length instrumental in getting the street paved with stone between the market and the brick foot pavement, that was

charity.   The names of the original contributors are likewise printed in this pamphlet, and among them is that of Franklin.   The pre-liminary arrangements were completed, and the first managers were elected, on the 1st of July, 1751.—ED.

on the side next the houses. This, for some time, gave an easy access to the market dry-shod; but, the rest of the street not being paved, whenever a carriage came out of the mud upon this pavement, it shook off and left its dirt upon it, and it was soon covered with mire, which was not removed, the city as yet having no scavengers.

After some inquiry, I found a poor industrious man, who was willing to undertake keeping the pavement clean, by sweeping it twice a week, carrying off the dirt from before all the neighbours' doors, for the sum of sixpence per month, to be paid by each house. I then wrote and printed a paper setting forth the advantages to the neighbourhood, that might be obtained from this small expense; the greater ease in keeping our houses clean, so much dirt not being brought in by people's feet; the benefit to the shops by more custom, as buyers could more easily get at them; and by not having in windy weather the dust blown in upon their goods, &c., &c. I sent one of these papers to each house, and in a day or two went round to see who would subscribe an agreement to pay these sixpences; it was unanimously signed, and for a time well executed. All the inhabitants of the city were delighted with the cleanliness of the pavement that surrounded the market, it being a convenience to all, and this raised a general desire to have all the streets paved; and made the people more willing to submit to a tax for that purpose.

After some time I drew a bill for paving the city, and brought it into the Assembly. It was just before I went to England, in 1757, and did not pass till I was gone, and then with an alteration in the mode of assessment, which I thought not for the better; but with an additional provision for lighting as well as paving the streets, which was a great improvement. It was by a private person, the late Mr. John Clifton, giving a sample of the utility of lamps, by placing one at his door, that the people were first impressed with the idea of lighting all the city. The honour of this public benefit has also been ascribed to me, but it belongs truly to that gentleman. I did but follow his example, and have only some merit to claim respecting the form of our lamps, as differing from the globe lamps, we were at first supplied with from London. They were found inconvenient in these respects; they admitted no air below; the smoke therefore did not readily go out above, but circulated in the globe, lodged on its inside, and soon obstructed the light they were intended to afford; giving besides the daily trouble of wiping them clean; and an accidental stroke on one of them would demolish it, and render it totally useless. I therefore suggested the composing them of four flat panes, with a long funnel above to draw up the smoke, and crevices admitting the air below to facilitate the ascent of the smoke; by this means they were kept clean, and did not grow dark in a few hours, as the London lamps do, but continued bright till morning; and an accidental stroke would generally break but a single pane, easily repaired.

I have sometimes wondered that the Londoners did not, from the effect holes in the bottom of the globe lamps used at Vauxhall have in keeping them clean, learn to have such holes in their street lamps. But, these holes being made for another purpose, viz., to communicate flame more suddenly to the wick by a little flax hanging down through them, the other use, of letting in air, seems not to have been thought of; and therefore, after the lamps have been lit a few hours, the streets of London are very poorly illuminated.

The mention of these improvements puts me in mind of one I proposed, when in London, to Dr. Fothergill, who was among the best men I have known, and a great promoter of useful projects. I had observed, that the streets, when dry, were never swept, and the light dust carried away; but it was suffered to accumulate till wet weather reduced it to mud; and then, after lying some days so deep on the pavement that there was no crossing but in paths kept clean by poor people with brooms, it was with great labour raked together and thrown up into carts, open above, the sides of which suffered some of the slush at every jolt on the pavement to shake out and fall; sometimes to the annoyance of foot passengers. The reason given for not sweeping the dusty streets was, that the dust would fly into the windows of shops and houses.

An accidental occurrence had instructed me how much sweeping might be done in a little time. I found at my door in Craven street, one morning, a poor woman sweeping my pavement with a birch-broom; she appeared very pale and feeble, as just come out of a fit of sickness. I asked who employed her to sweep there; she said, "Nobody; but I am poor and in distress, and I sweeps before gentlefolkeses doors, and hopes they will give me something." I bid her sweep the whole street clean, and I would give her a shilling; this was at nine o'clock; and at noon she came for the shilling.

From the slowness I saw at first in her working, I could scarce believe that the work was done so soon, and sent my servant to examine it, who reported that the whole street was swept perfectly clean, and all the dust placed in the gutter which was in the middle; and the next rain washed it quite away, so that the pavement and even the kennel were perfectly clean.

I then judged, that, if that feeble woman could sweep such a street in three hours, a strong active man might have done it in half the time. And here let me remark, the convenience of having but one gutter in such a narrow street running down its middle instead of two, one on each side near the footway. For where all the rain that falls on a street runs from the sides and meets in the middle, it forms there a current strong enough to wash away all the mud it meets with; but when divided into two channels, it is often too weak to cleanse either, and only makes the mud it finds more fluid; so that the wheels of carriages and feet of horses throw and dash it upon the foot pavement, which is thereby rendered foul and slippery, and sometimes splash it upon those who are walking. My proposal, communicated to the Doctor, was as follows;

" For the more effectually cleaning and keeping clean the streets of London and Westminster, it is proposed, that the several watchmen be contracted with to have the dust swept up in dry seasons, and the mud raked up at other times, each in the several streets and lanes of his round; that they be furnished with brooms and other proper instruments for these purposes, to be kept at their respective stands, ready to furnish the poor people they may employ in the service.

" That in the dry summer months the dust be all swept up into heaps at proper distances, before the shops and windows of houses are usually opened; when scavengers, with close covered carts, shall also carry it all away.

" That the mud, when raked up, be not left in heaps to be spread abroad again by the wheels of carriages and trampling of horses; but that the scavengers be provided with bodies of carts, not placed high upon wheels, but low upon sliders, with lattice bottoms, which, being covered with straw, will retain the mud thrown into them, and permit the water to drain from it; whereby it will become much lighter, water making the greatest part of the weight. These bodies of carts to be placed at convenient distances, and the mud brought to them in wheelbarrows; they remaining where placed till the mud is drained, and then horses brought to draw them away."

I have since had doubts of the practicability of the latter part of this proposal, in all places, on account of the narrowness of some streets, and the difficulty of placing the draining sleds so as not to encumber too much the passage; but I am still of opinion, that the former, requiring the dust to be swept up and carried away before the shops are open, is very practicable in the summer, when the days are long; for, in walking through the Strand and Fleet Street one morning at seven o'clock, I observed there was not one shop open, though it had been daylight and the sun up above three hours; the inhabitants of London choosing voluntarily to live much by candle-light, and sleep by sunshine : and yet often complain, a little absurdly, of the duty on candles, and the high price of tallow.

Some may think these trifling matters not worth minding or relating; but, when they consider, that though dust blown into the eyes of a single person, or into a single shop in a windy day, is but of small importance, yet the great number of the instances in a populous city, and its frequent repetition, gives it weight and consequence, perhaps they will not censure very severely those, who bestow some attention to affairs of this seemingly low nature. Human felicity is produced not so much by great pieces of good fortune that seldom happen, as by little advantages that occur every day. Thus, if you teach a poor young man to shave himself, and keep his razor in order, you may contribute more to the happiness of his life than in giving him a thousand guineas. This sum may be soon spent, the regret only remaining of having foolishly consumed it; but in the other case, he escapes the frequent vexation of waiting for barbers, and of their sometimes dirty fingers, offensive breaths, and dull razors; he shaves when most convenient to him, and enjoys daily the pleasure of its being done with a good instrument. With these sentiments I have hazarded the few preceding pages, hoping they may afford hints, which some time or other may be useful to a city I love, having lived many years in it very happily, and perhaps to some of our towns in America.

Having been some time employed by the postmaster-general of America, as his comptroller in regulating several offices, and bringing the officers to account, I was, upon his death, in 1753, appointed jointly with Mr. William Hunter, to succeed him, by a commission from the postmaster-general in England. The American office had hitherto never paid any thing to that of Britain. We were to have six hundred pounds a year between us, if we could make that sum out of the profits of the office. To do this, a variety of improvements was necessary; some of these were inevitably at first expensive: so that in the first four years the office became above nine hundred pounds in debt to us. But it soon after began to repay us: and before I was displaced by a freak of the ministers, of which I shall speak hereafter, we had brought it to yield *three times* as much clear revenue to the crown, as the post-office of Ireland. Since that imprudent transaction, they have received from it—not one farthing!

The business of the post-office occasioned my taking a journey this year to New England, where the College of Cambridge, of their own motion, presented me with the degree of Master of Arts. Yale College in Connecticut had before made me a similar compliment. Thus, without studying in any College, I came to partake of their honours. They were conferred in consideration of my improvements and discoveries in the electric branch of natural philosophy.

CHAPTER X.

In 1754, war with France being again apprehended, a congress of commissioners from the different colonies was by an order of the Lords of Trade to be assembled at Albany; there to confer with the chiefs of the Six Nations, concerning the means of defending both their country and ours. Governor Hamilton having received this order acquainted the House with it, requesting they would furnish proper presents for the Indians, to be given on this occasion; and naming the Speaker (Mr. Norris) and myself to join Mr. John Penn and Mr. Secretary Peters as commissioners to act for Pennsylvania. The House approved the nomination, and provided the goods for the presents, though they did not much like treating out of the province; and we met the other commissioners at Albany about the middle of June.

In our way thither, I projected and drew up a plan for the union of all the colonies under one government, so far as might be necessary for defence, and other important general purposes. As we passed through New York, I had there shown my project to Mr. James Alexander and Mr. Kennedy, two gentlemen of great knowledge in public affairs; and, being fortified by their approbation, I ventured to lay it before the congress. It then appeared that several of the commissioners had formed plans of the same kind. A previous question was first taken, whether a union should be established, which passed in the affirmative unanimously. A committee was then appointed, one member from each colony, to consider the several plans and report. Mine happened to be preferred; and, with a few amendments, was accordingly reported.

By this plan the general government was to be administered by a President-general, appointed and supported by the Crown; and a grand council was to be chosen by the representatives of the people of the several colonies, met in their respective assemblies. The debates upon it in congress went on daily, hand in hand with the Indian business. Many objections and difficulties were started; but at length they were all overcome, and the plan was unanimously agreed to, and copies ordered to be transmitted to the Board of Trade and to the Assemblies of the several provinces. Its fate was singular; the Assemblies did not adopt it, as they all thought there was too much *prerogative* in it; and in England it was judged to have too much of the *democratic*. The Board of Trade did not approve it, nor recommend it for the approbation of His Majesty; but another scheme was formed, supposed to answer the same purpose better, whereby the governors of the provinces, with some members of their respective councils, were to meet and order the raising of troops, building of forts, &c., and to draw on the treasury of Great Britain for the expense, which was afterwards to be refunded by an Act of Parliament, laying a tax on America. My plan, with my reasons in support of it, is to be found among my political papers that were printed.

Being the winter following in Boston, I had much conversation with Governor Shirley upon both the plans. Part of what passed between us on this occasion may also be seen among those papers. The different and contrary reasons of dislike to my plan makes me suspect that it was really the true medium; and I am still of opinion it would have been happy for both sides if it had been adopted. The colonies so united would have been sufficiently strong to have defended themselves; there would then have been no need of troops from England: of course the subsequent pretext for taxing

America, and the bloody contest it occasioned, would have been avoided. But such mistakes are not new; history is full of the errors of states and princes.

> " Look round the habitable world, how few
> Know their own good, or, knowing it, pursue !"

Those who govern, having much business on their hands, do not generally like to take the trouble of considering and carrying into execution new projects. The best public measures are therefore seldom adopted from previous wisdom, but forced by the occasion.

The Governor of Pennsylvania, in sending it down to the Assembly, expressed his approbation of the plan, " as appearing to him to be drawn up with great clearness and strength of judgment, and therefore recommended it as well worthy of their closest and most serious attention." The House, however, by the management of a certain member, took it up when I happened to be absent, which I thought not very fair, and reprobated it without paying any attention to it at all, to my no small mortification.

In my journey to Boston this year, I met at New York with our new Governor, Mr. Morris, just arrived there from England, with whom I had been before intimately acquainted. He brought a commission to supersede Mr. Hamilton, who, tired with the disputes his proprietary instructions subjected him to, had resigned. Mr. Morris asked me if I thought he must expect as uncomfortable an administration. I said, "No; you may on the contrary have a very comfortable one, if you will only take care not to enter into any dispute with the Assembly." "My dear friend," said he pleasantly, "how can you advise my avoiding disputes? You know I love disputing, it is one of my greatest pleasures; however, to show the regard I have for your counsel, I promise you I will, if possible, avoid them." He had some reason for loving to dispute: being eloquent, an acute sophister, and therefore generally successful in argumentative conversation. He had been brought up to it from a boy, his father, as I have heard, accustoming his children to dispute with one another for his diversion, while sitting at table after dinner; but I think the practice was not wise, for, in the course of my observation, those disputing, contradicting, and confuting people are generally unfortunate in their affairs. They get victory sometimes, but they never get goodwill, which would be of more use to them. We parted; he going to Philadelphia, and I to Boston.

In returning I met at New York with the votes of the Assembly of Pennsylvania, by which it appeared that, notwithstanding his promise to me, he and the House were already in high contention; and it was a continual battle between them as long as he retained the government. I had my share of it; for, as soon as I got back to my seat in the the Assembly, I was put on every committee for answering his speeches and messages, and by the committees always desired to make the drafts. Our answers, as well as his messages, were often tart and sometimes indecently abusive; and, as he knew I wrote for the Assembly, one might have imagined that when we met we could hardly avoid cutting throats. But he was so good-natured a man, that no personal difference between him and me was occasioned by the contest, and we often dined together.

One afternoon, in the height of this public quarrel, we met in the street. "Franklin," said he, "you must go home with me and spend the evening; I am to have some company that you will like;" and, taking me by the arm, led me to his house. In gay conversation over our wine after supper, he told us jokingly that he much admired the idea of Sancho Panza, who when it was proposed to give him a government, requested it might be a government of blacks; as then, if he could not agree with his people, he might sell them. One of his friends, who sat next to me, said, "Franklin, why do you continue to side with those damned Quakers? Had you not better sell them? The Proprietor would give you a good price." "The Governor," said I, "has not yet *blacked* them enough." He indeed had laboured hard to blacken the Assembly in all his messages, but they wiped off his colouring as fast as he laid it on, and placed it, in return, thick upon his own face; so that finding he was likely to be *negrofied* himself, he, as well as Mr. Hamilton, grew tired of the contest, and quitted the government.

These public quarrels were all at bottom owing to the Proprietaries, our hereditary governors; who when any expense was to be incurred for the defence of their province, with incredible meanness, instructed their deputies to pass no Act for levying the necessary taxes unless their vast estates were in the same Act expressly exonerated; and they had even taken the bonds of these deputies to observe such instructions. The Assemblies for three years held out against this injustice, though constrained to bend at last. At length

Captain Denny, who was Governor Morris's successor, ventured to disobey those instructions; how that was brought about I shall show hereafter.

But I am got forward too fast with my story; there are still some transactions to be mentioned that happened during the administration of Governor Morris.

War being in a manner commenced with France, the government of Massachusetts Bay projected an attack upon Crown Point, and sent Mr. Quincy to Pennsylvania, and Mr. Pownall, afterwards Governor Pownall, to New York, to solicit assistance. As I was in the Assembly, knew its temper, and was Mr. Quincy's countryman, he applied to me for my influence and assistance. I dictated his address to them, which was well received. They voted an aid of ten thousand pounds, to be laid out in provisions. But the Governor refusing his assent to their bill, (which included this with other sums granted for the use of the crown,) unless a clause were inserted, exempting the proprietary estate from bearing any part of the tax that would be necessary; the Assembly, though very desirous of making their grant to New England effectual, were at a loss how to accomplish it. Mr. Quincy laboured hard with the Governor to obtain his assent, but he was obstinate.

I then suggested a method of doing the business without the Governor, by orders on the trustees of the Loan Office, which by law the Assembly had the right of drawing. There was indeed little or no money at the time in the office, and, therefore, I proposed that the orders should be payable in a year, and to bear an interest of five per cent. With these orders I supposed the provisions might easily be purchased. The Assembly, with very little hesitation, adopted the proposal. The orders were immediately printed, and I was one of the committee directed to sign and dispose of them. The fund for paying them was the interest of all the paper currency then extant in the province upon loan, together with the revenue arising from the excise, which being known to be more than sufficient, they obtained credit, and were not only taken in payment for the provisions, but many moneyed people who had cash lying by them, vested it in those orders, which they found advantageous, as they bore interest while upon hand, and might on any occasion be used as money; so that they were eagerly all bought up, and in a few weeks none of them was to be seen. Thus this important affair was by my means completed. Mr. Quincy returned thanks to the Assembly in a handsome memorial, went home highly pleased with the success of his embassy, and ever after bore for me the most cordial and affectionate friendship.

The British government, not choosing to permit the union of the colonies as proposed at Albany, and to trust that union with their defence, lest they should thereby grow too military, and feel their own strength, suspicion and jealousies at this time being entertained of them, sent over General Braddock, with two regiments of regular English troops for that purpose. He landed at Alexandria in Virginia, and thence marched to Frederictown in Maryland, where he halted for carriages. Our Assembly apprehending, from some information, that he had received violent prejudices against them, as averse to the service, wished me to wait upon him, not as from them, but as postmaster-general, under the guise of proposing to settle with him the mode of conducting with most celerity and certainty the despatches between him and the governors of the several provinces, with whom he must necessarily have continual correspondence, and of which they proposed to pay the expense. My son accompanied me on this journey,

We found the General at Frederictown, waiting impatiently for the return of those he had sent through the back parts of Maryland and Virginia to collect wagons. I stayed with him several days, dined with him daily, and had full opportunities of removing his prejudices, by the information of what the Assembly had before his arrival actually done, and were still willing to do, to facilitate his operations. When I was about to depart, the returns of wagons to be obtained were brought in, by which it appeared that they amounted only to twenty-five, and not all of those were in serviceable condition. The General and all the officers were surprised, declared the expedition was then at an end, being impossible, and exclaimed against the ministers for ignorantly sending them into a country destitute of the means of conveying their stores, baggage, &c., not less than one hundred and fifty wagons being necessary.

I happened to say, I thought it was a pity they had not been landed in Pennsylvania, as in that country almost every farmer had his wagon. The General eagerly laid hold of my words, and said, " Then you, Sir, who are a man of interest there, can probably procure them for us, and I beg you will undertake it." I asked what terms were to be offered the owners of the wagons, and I was desired to put on paper the terms that appeared to me necessary. This I did, and they were agreed to, and a commission and instructions accordingly prepared immediately. What those terms were will appear in the advertisement I published as soon as I arrived at Lancaster, which being, from the great and sudden effect it produced, a piece of some curiosity, I shall insert it at length as follows:—

"ADVERTISEMENT.

"Lancaster, April 26th, 1755.

"Whereas, one hundred and fifty wagons, with four horses to each wagon, and fifteen hundred saddle or pack-horses, are wanted for the service of his Majesty's forces, now about to rendezvous at Will's Creek; and his Excellency General Braddock having been pleased to empower me to contract for the hire of the same; I hereby give notice, that I shall attend for that purpose, at Lancaster, from this day to next Wednesday evening; and at York, from next Thursday morning, till Friday evening; where I shall be ready to agree for wagons and teams, or single horses, on the following terms; viz. 1. That there shall be paid for each wagon, with four good horses and a driver, fifteen shillings *per diem;* and for each able horse with a pack-saddle, or other saddle and furniture, two shillings *per diem;* and for each able horse without a saddle, eighteen pence *per diem.* 2. That the pay commence from the time of their joining the forces, at Will's Creek, which must be on or before the 20th of May ensuing, and that a reasonable allowance be paid over and above, for the time necessary for their travelling to Will's Creek, and home again after their discharge. 3. Each wagon and team, and every saddle or pack-horse is to be valued by indifferent persons, chosen between me and the owner; and, in case of the loss of any wagon, team, or other horse in the service, the price according to such valuation is to be allowed and paid. 4. Seven days' pay is to be advanced and paid in hand by me to the owner of each wagon and team, or horse, at the time of contracting, if required; and the remainder to be paid by General Braddock, or by the paymaster of the army, at the time of their discharge; or from time to time, as it shall be demanded. 5. No drivers of wagons, or persons taking care of the hired horses, are on any account to be called upon to do the duty of soldiers, or be otherwise employed than in conducting or taking care of their carriages or horses. 6. All oats, Indian corn, or other forage, that wagons or horses bring to the camp, more than is necessary for the subsistence of the horses, is to be taken for the use of the army, and a reasonable price paid for the same.

"*Note.*—My son, William Franklin, is empowered to enter into like contracts with any person in Cumberland County.   B. FRANKLIN."

"*To the Inhabitants of the Counties of Lancaster, York, and Cumberland.*

"Friends and Countrymen,

"Being occasionally at the camp at Frederic a few days since, I found the General and officers extremely exasperated on account of their not being supplied with horses and carriages, which had been expected from this province, as most able to furnish them ; but, through the dissensions between our Governor and Assembly, money had not been provided, nor any steps taken for that purpose.

"It was proposed to send an armed force immediately into these counties, to seize as many of the best carriages and horses as should be wanted, and compel as many persons into the service as would be necessary to drive and take care of them.

"I apprehended, that the progress of British soldiers through these counties on such an occasion, especially considering the temper they are in, and their resentment against us, would be attended with many and great inconveniences to the inhabitants, and therefore more willingly took the trouble of trying first what might be done by fair and equitable means. The people of these back counties have lately complained, to the Assembly, that a sufficient currency was wanting; you have an opportunity of receiving and dividing among you a very considerable sum; for, if the service of this expedition should continue, as it is more than probable it will, for one hundred and twenty days, the hire of these waggons and horses will amount to upwards of thirty thousand pounds; which will be paid you in silver and gold, of the King's money.

"The service will be light and easy, for the army will scarce march above twelve miles per day, and the wagons and baggage horses, as they carry those things that are absolutely necessary to the welfare of the army, must march with the army, and no faster ; and are, for the army's sake, always placed where they can be most secure, whether in a march or in a camp.

"If you are really, as I believe you are, good and loyal subjects to his Majesty, you may now do a most acceptable service, and make it easy to yourselves ; for three or four of such as cannot separately spare from the business of their plantations, a wagon and four horses and a driver, may do it together; one furnishing the wagon, another one or two horses, and another the driver, and divide the pay proportionably between you. But, if you do not this service to your King and country voluntarily, when such good pay and reasonable terms are offered to you, your loyalty will be strongly suspected. The King's business must be done ; so many brave troops, come so far for your defence, must not stand idle through your backwardness to do what may be reasonably expected from you ; wagons and horses must be had ; violent measures will probably be used ; and you will be left to seek for a recompense where you can find it, and your case perhaps be little pitied or regarded.

"I have no particular interest in this affair, as, except the satisfaction of endeavouring to do good, I shall have only my labour for my pains. If this method of obtaining the wagons and horses is not likely to succeed, I am obliged to send word to the General in fourteen days; and I suppose Sir John St. Clair, the hussar, with a body of soldiers, will immediately enter the province for the purpose ; which I shall be sorry to hear, because I am very sincerely and truly your friend and well-wisher,   "B. FRANKLIN."

I received of the General about eight hundred pounds, to be disbursed in advance money to the wagon owners ; but,

that sum being insufficient, I advanced upwards of two
hundred pounds more ; and in two weeks the one hundred
and fifty wagons, with two hundred and fifty-nine carrying
horses, were on their march for the camp. The advertisement promised payment according to the valuation, in case
any waggons or horses should be lost. The owners, however,
alleging they did not know General Braddock, or what dependence might be had on his promise, insisted on my bond
for the performance; which I accordingly gave them.

While I was at the camp, supping one evening with the
officers of Colonel Dunbar's regiment, he represented to me
his concern for the subalterns, who, he said, were generally
not in affluence, and could ill afford in this dear country to
lay in the stores that might be necessary in so long a march
through a wilderness, where nothing was to be purchased. I
commiserated their case, and resolved to endeavour procuring
them some relief. I said nothing, however, to him of my intention, but wrote the next morning to the Committee of the
Assembly, who had the disposition of some public money,
warmly recommending the case of these officers to their consideration, and proposing that a present should be sent them
of necessaries and refreshments. My son, who had some
experience of a camp life, and of its wants, drew up a list for
me, which I inclosed in my letter. The committee approved,
and used such diligence, that, conducted by my son, the
stores arrived at the camp as soon as the wagons. They
consisted of twenty parcels, each containing

6lbs. loaf sugar.	1 Gloucester cheese.
6 do. Muscovado do.	1 keg containing 20lbs. good butter.
1 do. green tea.	2 dozen old Madeira wine.
1 do. bohea do.	2 gallons Jamaica spirits.
6 do. ground coffee.	1 bottle flour of mustard.
6 do. chocolate.	2 well-cured hams.
½ chest best white biscuit.	½ dozen dried tongues.
½lb. pepper.	6lbs. rice.
1 quart white vinegar.	6lbs. raisins.

These parcels, well packed, were placed on as many horses,
each parcel, with the horse, being intended as a present for
one officer. They were very thankfully received, and the
kindness acknowledged by letters to me, from the colonels of
both regiments, in the most grateful terms. The General too
was highly satisfied with **my** conduct in procuring him the
waggons, and readily paid my account of disbursements ;
thanking me repeatedly, and requesting my further assist-

ance in sending provisions after him. I undertook this also, and was busily employed in it till we heard of his defeat; advancing for the service, of my own money, upwards of one thousand pounds sterling; of which I sent him an account. It came to his hands, luckily for me, a few days before the battle, and he returned me immediately an order on the paymaster for the round sum of one thousand pounds, leaving the remainder to the next account. I consider this payment as good luck, having never been able to obtain that remainder; of which more hereafter.

This General was, I think, a brave man, and might probably have made a figure as a good officer in some European war. But he had too much self-confidence, too high an opinion of the validity of regular troops, and too mean a one of both Americans and Indians. George Croghan, our Indian interpreter, joined him on his march with one hundred of those people, who might have been of great use to his army as guides and scouts, if he had treated them kindly; but he slighted and neglected them, and they gradually left him.

In conversation with him one day, he was giving me some account of his intended progress. "After taking Fort Duquesne," said he, "I am to proceed to Niagara; and, having taken that, to Frontenac, if the season will allow time, and I suppose it will; for Duquesne can hardly detain me above three or four days; and then I see nothing that can obstruct my march to Niagara." Having before revolved in my mind the long line his army must make in their march by a very narrow road, to be cut for them through the woods and bushes, and also what I had read of a former defeat of fifteen hundred French, who invaded the Illinois country, I had conceived some doubts and some fears for the event of the campaign. But I ventured only to say, "To be sure, Sir, if you arrive well before Duquesne, with these fine troops, so well provided with artillery, the fort, though completely fortified, and assisted with a very strong garrison, can probably make but a short resistance. The only danger I apprehend of obstruction to your march, is from the ambuscades of the Indians, who, by constant practice, are dexterous in laying and executing them; and the slender line, near four miles long, which your army must make, may expose it to be attacked by surprise in its flanks, and to be cut like a thread into several pieces, which, from their distance cannot come up in time to support each other."

K 2

He smiled at my ignorance, and replied, "These savages may indeed be a formidable enemy to your raw American militia: but upon the King's regular and disciplined troops, Sir, it is impossible they should make any impression." I was conscious of an impropriety in my disputing with a military man in matters of his profession, and said no more. The enemy, however, did not take the advantage of his army, which I apprehended its long line of march exposed it to, but let it advance without interruption till within nine miles of the place; and then, when more in a body, (for it had just passed a river, where the front had halted till all were come over,) and in a more open part of the woods than any it had passed, attacked its advanced guard by a heavy fire from behind trees and bushes; which was the first intelligence the General had of an enemy's being near him. This guard being disordered, the General hurried the troops up to their assistance, which was done in great confusion through wagons, baggage, and cattle; and presently the fire came upon their flank; the officers being on horseback were more easily distinguished, picked out as marks, and fell very fast; and the soldiers were crowded together in a huddle, having or hearing no orders, and standing to be shot at till two-thirds of them were killed; and then, being seized with a panic, the remainder fled with precipitation.

The wagoners took each a horse out of his team and scampered; their example was immediately followed by others; so that all the wagons, provisions, artillery, and stores, were left to the enemy. The General, being wounded, was brought off with difficulty; his secretary, Mr. Shirley, was killed by his side, and out of eighty-six officers sixty-three were killed or wounded; and seven hundred and fourteen men killed of eleven hundred. These eleven hundred had been picked men from the whole army; the rest had been left behind with Colonel Dunbar, who was to follow with the heavier part of the stores, provisions, and baggage. The flyers, not being pursued, arrived at Dunbar's camp, and the panic they brought with them instantly seized him and all his people. And, though he had now above one thousand men, and the enemy who had beaten Braddock did not at most exceed four hundred Indians and French together, instead of proceeding, and endeavouring to recover some of the lost honour, he ordered all the stores, ammunition, &c., to be destroyed, that he might have more horses to assist his flight towards the settlements, and less lumber to remove. He was there met with requests from the governors of Virginia, Maryland, and Pennsylvania, that he would post his troops on the frontiers, so as to afford some protection to the inhabitants; but he continued his hasty march through all the country, not thinking himself safe till he arrived at Philadelphia, where the inhabitants could protect him. This whole transaction gave us Americans the first suspicion, that our exalted ideas of the prowess of British regular troops had not been well founded.*

In their first march, too, from their landing till they got beyond the settlements, they had plundered and stripped the inhabitants, totally ruining some poor families, besides insulting, abusing, and confining the people, if they remonstrated. This was enough to put us out of conceit of such defenders, if we had really wanted any. How different was the conduct of our French friends in 1781, who, during a march through the most inhabited part of our country, from Rhode Island to Virginia, near seven hundred miles, occasioned not the smallest complaint for the loss of a pig, a chicken, or even an apple.

Captain Orme, who was one of the General's aides-de-camp, and, being grievously wounded, was brought off with him, and continued with him to his death, which happened in a few days, told me, that he was totally silent all the first day, and at night only said, " Who would have thought it ?" That he was silent again the following day, saying only at last, " We shall better know how to deal with them another time;" and died in a few minutes after.

The secretary's papers, with all the General's orders, instructions, and correspondence, falling into the enemy's hands, they selected and translated into French a number of the articles, which they printed, to prove the hostile intentions of the British court before the declaration of war. Among these I saw some letters of the General to the ministry, speaking highly of the great service I had rendered the army, and recommending me to their notice. David Hume, who was some years afterwards secretary to Lord Hertford, when minister in France, and afterwards to General Conway, when Secretary of State, told me he had seen among the papers in that office letters from Braddock, highly recommending me. But the expedition having been unfortunate, my service,

---

* There are some errors in this account of Braddock's defeat. A full description of that event may be seen in *Washington's Writings,* Vol. II. p. 468.—ED.

it seems, was not thought of much value, for those recommendations were never of any use to me.

As to rewards from himself, I asked only one, which was, that he would give orders to his officers not to enlist any more of our bought servants, and that he would discharge such as had been already enlisted. This he readily granted, and several were accordingly returned to their masters, on my application. Dunbar, when the command devolved on him, was not so generous. He being at Philadelphia, on his retreat, or rather flight, I applied to him for the discharge of the servants of three poor farmers of Lancaster County, that he had enlisted, reminding him of the late General's orders on that head. He promised me that if the masters would come to him at Trenton, where he should be in a few days on his march to New York, he would there deliver their men to them. They accordingly were at the expense and trouble of going to Trenton, and there he refused to perform his promise, to their great loss and disappointment.

As soon as the loss of the wagons and horses was generally known, all the owners came upon me for the valuation which I had given bond to pay. Their demands gave me a great deal of trouble. I acquainted them that the money was ready in the paymaster's hands, but the order for paying it must first be obtained from General Shirley, and that I had applied for it, but he being at a distance an answer could not soon be received, and they must have patience. All this, however, was not sufficient to satisfy them, and some began to sue me. General Shirley at length relieved me from this terrible situation, by appointing commissioners to examine the claims, and ordering payment. They amounted to near twenty thousand pounds, which to pay would have ruined me.

Before we had the news of this defeat, the two Doctors Bond came to me with a subscription paper for raising money to defray the expense of a grand firework, which it was intended to exhibit at a rejoicing on receiving the news of our taking Fort Duquesne. I looked grave, and said it would, I thought, be time enough to prepare the rejoicing when we knew we should have occasion to rejoice. They seemed surprised that I did not immediately comply with their proposal. "Why the d—l!" said one of them, "you surely don't suppose that the fort will not be taken?" "I don't know that it will not be taken; but I know that the events of war are subject to great uncertainty." I gave them the reasons of my doubting; the subscription was dropped, and the projectors thereby missed the mortification they would have undergone if the firework had been prepared. Dr. Bond, on some other occasion afterwards, said that he did not like Franklin's forebodings.

CHAPTER XI.

GOVERNOR MORRIS, who had continually worried the Assembly with message after message before the defeat of Braddock, to beat them into the making of Acts to raise money for the defence of the province, without taxing among others the proprietary estates, and had rejected all their Bills for not having such an exempting clause, now redoubled his attacks with more hope of success, the danger and necessity being greater. The Assembly, however, continued firm, believing they had justice on their side, and that it would be giving up an essential right if they suffered the Governor to amend their money bills. In one of the last, indeed, which was for granting fifty thousand pounds, his proposed amendment was only of a single word. The Bill expressed, "that all estates real and personal were to be taxed; those of the Proprietaries *not* excepted." His amendment was; for *not*, read *only*. A small, but very material alteration. However, when the news of the disaster reached England, our friends there, whom we had taken care to furnish with all the Assembly's answers to the Governor's messages, raised a clamour against the Proprietaries for their meanness and injustice in giving their Governor such instructions; some going so far as to say, that by obstructing the defence of their province, they forfeited their right to it. They were intimidated by this, and sent orders to their Receiver-General to add five thousand pounds of their money to whatever sum might be given by the Assembly for such purpose.

This, being testified to the House, was accepted in lieu of their share of a general tax; and a new Bill was formed with an exempting clause, which passed accordingly. By this Act I was appointed one of the commissioners for disposing of the money—sixty thousand pounds. I had been active in modelling the Bill and procuring its passage, and had at the same time drawn one for establishing and disciplining a voluntary militia; which I carried through the House without much difficulty, as care was taken in it to leave the Quakers at liberty. To promote the association necessary to form tha

militia, I wrote a Dialogue stating and answering all the
objections I could think of to such a militia; which was
printed, and had, as I thought, great effect.

While the several companies in the city and country were
forming, and learning their exercise, the Governor prevailed
with me to take charge of our north-western frontier, which
was infested by the enemy, and provide for the defence of the
inhabitants by raising troops and building a line of forts. I
undertook this military business, though I did not conceive
myself well qualified for it. He gave me a commission with
full powers, and a parcel of blank commissions for officers, to
be given to whom I thought fit. I had but little difficulty in
raising men, having soon five hundred and sixty under my
command. My son, who had in the preceding war been an
officer in the army raised against Canada, was my aide-de-
camp, and of great use to me. The Indians had burned
Gnadenhutten, a village settled by the Moravians, and massacred the inhabitants; but the place was thought a good
situation for one of the forts.

In order to march thither, I assembled the companies at
Bethlehem, the chief establishment of these people. I was
surprised to find it in so good a posture of defence; the
destruction of Gnadenhutten had made them apprehend
danger. The principal buildings were defended by a
stockade; they had purchased a quantity of arms and ammunition from New York, and had even placed quantities of
small paving stones between the windows of their high
stone houses, for their women to throw them down upon
the heads of any Indians that should attempt to force into
them. The armed brethren, too, kept watch and relieved
each other on guard, as methodically as in any garrison town.
In conversation with the Bishop, Spangenberg, I mentioned
my surprise; for, knowing they had obtained an Act of Parliament exempting them from military duties in the colonies,
I had supposed they were conscientiously scrupulous of
bearing arms. He answered me, that it was not one of their
established principles; but that, at the time of their obtaining
that Act, it was thought to be a principle with many of their
people. On this occasion, however, they to their surprise
found it adopted by but a few. It seems they were either
deceived in themselves, or deceived the Parliament; but
common sense, aided by present danger, will sometimes be
too strong for whimsical opinions.

It was the beginning of January when we set out upon this business of building forts. I sent one detachment towards the Minisink, with instructions to erect one for the security of that upper part of the country; and another to the lower part, with similar instructions; and I concluded to go myself with the rest of my force to Gnadenhutten, where a fort was thought more immediately necessary. The Moravians procured me five wagons for our tools, stores, and baggage.

Just before we had left Bethlehem, eleven farmers, who had been driven from their plantations by the Indians, came to me requesting a supply of fire-arms, that they might go back and bring off their cattle. I gave them each a gun with suitable ammunition. We had not marched many miles, before it began to rain, and it continued raining all day; there were no habitations on the road to shelter us, till we arrived near night at the house of a German, where, and in his barn, we were all huddled together, as wet as water could make us. It was well we were not attacked in our march, for our arms were of the most ordinary sort, and our men could not keep the locks of their guns dry. The Indians are dexterous in contrivances for that purpose, which we had not. They met that day the eleven poor farmers above mentioned, and killed ten of them. The one that escaped informed us, that his and his companions' guns would not go off, the priming being wet with the rain.

The next day being fair, we continued our march, and arrived at the desolated Gnadenhutten. There was a mill near, round which were left several pine boards, with which we soon hutted ourselves; an operation the more necessary at that inclement season, as we had no tents. Our first work was to bury more effectually the dead we found there, who had been half interred by the country people.

The next morning our fort was planned and marked out, the circumference measuring four hundred and fifty-five feet, which would require as many palisades to be made, one with another, of a foot diameter each. Our axes, of which we had seventy, were immediately set to work to cut down trees; and, our men being dexterous in the use of them, great despatch was made. Seeing the trees fall so fast, I had the curiosity to look at my watch when two men began to cut at a pine; in six minutes they had it upon the ground, and I found it of fourteen inches diameter. Each pine made three palisades of eighteen feet long, pointed at one end. While these were preparing, our other men dug a trench all round, of three feet deep, in which the palisades were to be planted; and, the bodies being taken off our wagons, and the fore and hind wheels separated, by taking out the pin which united the two parts of the perch, we had ten carriages, with two horses each, to bring the palisades from the woods to the spot. When they were set up, our carpenters built a platform of boards all round within, about six feet high, for the men to stand on when to fire through the loop holes. We had one swivel gun, which we mounted on one of the angles, and fired it as soon as fixed, to let the Indians know, if any were within hearing, that we had such pieces; and thus our fort, if that name may be given to so miserable a stockade, was finished in a week, though it rained so hard every other day, that the men could not work.

This gave me occasion to observe, that, when men are employed, they are best contented; for on the days they worked they were good-natured and cheerful, and, with the consciousness of having done a good day's work, they spent the evening jollily; but on our idle days they were mutinous and quarrelsome, finding fault with the pork, the bread, &c., and were continually in bad humour; which put me in mind of a sea captain, whose rule it was to keep his men constantly at work; and when his mate once told him, that they had done everything, and there was nothing further to employ them about; " Oh!" said he, " make them scour the anchor."

This kind of fort, however contemptible, is a sufficient defence against Indians, who have no cannon. Finding ourselves now posted securely, and having a place to retreat to on occasion, we ventured out in parties to scour the adjacent country. We met with no Indians, but we found the places on the neighbouring hills, where they had lain to watch our proceedings. There was an art in their contrivance of those places, that seems worth mentioning. It being winter, a fire was necessary for them; but a common fire on the surface of the ground would by its light have discovered their position at a distance. They had therefore dug holes in the ground about three feet diameter, and somewhat deeper; we found where they had with their hatchets cut off the charcoal from the sides of burnt logs lying in the woods. With these coals they had made small fires in the bottom of the holes, and we observed among the weeds and grass the prints of their bodies, made by their lying all round with their legs hanging down in the holes to keep their feet warm ; which with them is an essential point. This kind of fire so managed could not discover them either by its light, flame, sparks, or even smoke ; it appeared that the number was not great, and it seems they saw we were too many to be attacked by them with prospect of advantage.

We had for our chaplain a zealous Presbyterian minister, Mr. Beatty, who complained to me that the men did not generally attend his prayers and exhortations. When they enlisted they were promised, besides pay and provisions, a gill of rum a day, which was punctually served out to them, half in the morning and the other half in the evening, and I observed they were punctual in attending to receive it ; upon which I said to Mr. Beatty, " It is perhaps below the dignity of your profession to act as steward of the rum, but if you were only to distribute it out after prayers you would have them all about you." He liked the thought, undertook the task, and, with the help of a few hands to measure out the liquor, executed it to satisfaction, and never were prayers more generally and more punctually attended. So that I think this method preferable to the punishment inflicted by some military laws for non-attendance on divine service.

I had hardly finished this business and got my fort well stored with provisions when I received a letter from the Governor, acquainting me that he had called the Assembly, and wished my attendance there if the posture of affairs on the frontiers was such that my remaining there was no longer necessary. My friends, too, of the Assembly pressing me by their letters to be, if possible, at the meeting, and my three intended forts being now completed and the inhabitants contented to remain on their farms under that protection, I resolved to return ; the more willingly as a New England officer, Colonel Clapham, experienced in Indian war, being on a visit to our establishment, consented to accept the command. I gave him a commission, and, parading the garrison, had it read before them, and introduced him to them as an officer who, from his skill in military affairs, was much more fit to command them than myself, and giving them a little exhortation, took my leave. I was escorted as far as Bethlehem, where I rested a few days to recover from the fatigue I had undergone. The first night, lying in a good bed, I could hardly sleep, it was so different from my hard lodging on the floor of a hut at Gnadenhutten with only a blanket or two.

While at Bethlehem, I inquired a little into the practices of the Moravians; some of them had accompanied me, and all were very kind to me. I found they worked for a common stock, ate at common tables, and slept in common dormitories, great numbers together. In the dormitories I observed loopholes, at certain distances all along just under the ceiling, which I thought judiciously placed for change of air. I went to their church, where I was entertained with good music, the organ being accompanied with violins, hautboys, flutes, clarinets, &c. I understood their sermons were not usually preached to mixed congregations of men, women, and children, as is our common practice; but that they assembled sometimes the married men, at other times their wives, then the young men, the young women, and the little children; each division by itself. The sermon I heard was to the latter, who came in, and were placed in rows on benches; the boys under the conduct of a young man, their tutor, and the girls conducted by a young woman. The discourse seemed well adapted to their capacities, and was delivered in a pleasing, familiar manner, coaxing them, as it were, to be good. They behaved very orderly, but looked pale and unhealthy; which made me suspect they were kept too much within doors or not allowed sufficient exercise.

I inquired concerning the Moravian marriages, whether the report was true that they were by lot. I was told that lots were used only in particular cases; that generally when a young man found himself disposed to marry, he informed the elders of his class, who consulted the elder ladies that governed the young women. As these elders of the different sexes were well acquainted with the tempers and dispositions of their respective pupils they could best judge what matches were suitable, and their judgments were generally acquiesced in. But if, for example, it should happen that two or three young women were found to be equally proper for the young man, the lot was then recurred to. I objected if the matches are not made by the mutual choice of the parties, some of them may chance to be very unhappy. "And so they may," answered my informer, "if you let the parties choose for themselves." Which indeed I could not deny.

Being returned to Philadelphia, I found the Association went on with great success. The inhabitants, that were not Quakers, having pretty generally come into it, formed themselves into companies, and chose their captains, lieutenants, and ensigns, according to the new law. Dr. Bond visited me, and gave me an account of the pains he had taken to spread a general good liking to the law, and ascribed much to those endeavours.   I had the vanity to ascribe all to my *Dialogue;* however, not knowing but that he might be in the right, I let him enjoy his opinion; which I take to be generally the best way in such cases.   The officers, meeting, chose me to be colonel of the regiment, which I this time accepted.   I forget how many companies we had, but we paraded about twelve hundred well-looking men, with a company of artillery, who had been furnished with six brass field-pieces, which they had become so expert in the use of, as to fire twelve times in a minute.   The first time I reviewed my regiment they accompanied me to my house, and would salute me with some rounds fired before my door, which shook down and broke several glasses of my electrical apparatus. And my new honour proved not much less brittle; for all our commissions were soon after broken, by a repeal of the law in England.

During this short time of my colonelship, being about to set out on a journey to Virginia, the officers of my regiment took it into their heads, that it would be proper for them to escort me out of town, as far as the Lower Ferry.   Just as I was getting on horseback they came to my door, between thirty and forty, mounted, and all in their uniforms.   I had not been previously acquainted with their project, or I should have prevented it, being naturally averse to the assuming of state on any occasion ; and I was a good deal chagrined at their appearance, as I could not avoid their accompanying me.   What made it worse was, that, as soon as we began to move, they drew their swords and rode with them naked all the way.   Somebody wrote an account of this to the Proprietor, and it gave him great offence.   No such honour had been paid to him, when in the province ; nor to any of his governors ; and he said, it was only proper to princes of the blood royal ; which may be true for aught I know, who was, and still am, ignorant of the etiquette in such cases.

This silly affair, however, greatly increased his rancour against me, which was before considerable on account of my conduct in the Assembly respecting the exemption of his estate from taxation, which I had always opposed very warmly, and not without severe reflections on the meanness and injustice of contending for it.   He accused me to the ministry, as being the great obstacle to the King's service,

preventing by my influence in the House the proper form
of the bills for raising money; and he instanced the parade
with my officers, as a proof of my having an intention to take
the government of the province out of his hands by force.
He also applied to Sir Everard Fawkener, the Postmaster
general, to deprive me of my office.   But it had no other effect
than to procure from Sir Everard a gentle admonition.

Notwithstanding the continual wrangle between the Governor and the House, in which I as a member had so large
a share, there still subsisted a civil intercourse between that
gentleman and myself, and we never had any personal difference.   I have sometimes since thought, that his little or no
resentment against me, for the answers it was known I drew
up to his messages, might be the effect of professional habit,
and that, being bred a lawyer, he might consider us both as
merely advocates for contending clients in a suit; he for the
Proprietaries, and I for the Assembly.   He would therefore
sometimes call in a friendly way to advise with me on difficult
points; and sometimes, though not often, take my advice.

We acted in concert to supply Braddock's army with provisions; and, when the shocking news arrived of his defeat,
the Governor sent in haste for me, to consult with him on
measures for preventing the desertion of the back counties.
I forget now the advice I gave; but I think it was, that
Dunbar should be written to, and prevailed with, if possible,
to post his troops on the frontiers for their protection, until,
by reinforcements from the colonies, he might be able to
proceed in the expedition.   And, after my return from the
frontier, he would have had me undertake the conduct of such
an expedition with provincial troops, for the reduction of Fort
Duquesne, Dunbar and his men being otherwise employed;
and he proposed to commission me as general.   I had not so
good an opinion of my military abilities as he professed to
have, and I believe his professions must have exceeded his
real sentiments; but probably he might think, that my popu-
larity would facilitate the business with the men, and influence
in the Assembly the grant of money to pay for it; and that
perhaps without taxing the Proprietary.   Finding me not so
forward to engage as he expected, the project was dropped;
and he soon after left the government, being superseded by
Captain Denny.

Before I proceed in relating the part I had in public affairs
under this new Governor's administration, it may not be amiss

to give here some account of the rise and progress of my phi-losophical reputation.

In 1746, being in Boston, I met there with a Dr. Spence, who was lately arrived from Scotland, and showed me some electric experiments. They were imperfectly performed, as he was not very expert; but, being on a subject quite new to me, they equally surprised and pleased me. Soon after my return to Philadelphia, our library company received from Mr. Peter Collinson, Fellow of the Royal Society of London, a present of a glass tube, with some account of the use of it in making such experiments. I eagerly seized the opportu-nity of repeating what I had seen at Boston; and, by much practice, acquired great readiness in performing those also, which we had an account of from England, adding a number of new ones. I say much practice, for my house was con-tinually full, for some time, with persons who came to see these new wonders.

To divide a little this incumbrance among my friends, I caused a number of similar tubes to be blown in our glass-house, with which they furnished themselves, so that we had at length several performers. Among these the principal was Mr. Kinnersley, an ingenious neighbour, who being out of business, I encouraged him to undertake showing the ex-periments for money, and drew up for him two lectures, in which the experiments were ranged in such order, and accom-panied with explanations in such method, as that the fore-going should assist in comprehending the following. He procured an elegant apparatus for the purpose, in which all the little machines that I had roughly made for myself were neatly formed by instrument makers. His lectures were well attended, and gave great satisfaction; and after some time he went through the colonies, exhibiting them in every capital town, and picked up some money. In the West India Islands, indeed, it was with difficulty the experiments could be made, from the general moisture of the air.

. Obliged as we were to Mr. Collinson for the present of the tube, &c., I thought it right he should be informed of our success in using it, and wrote him several letters containing accounts of our experiments. He got them read in the Royal Society, where they were not at first thought worth so much notice as to be printed in their *Transactions*. One paper, which I wrote for Mr. Kinnersley, on the sameness of lightning with electricity, I sent to Mr. Mitchel an acquaintance of mine, and one of the Members also of that Society, who wrote me word, that it had been read, but was laughed at by the connoisseurs. The papers, however, being shown to Dr. Fothergill, he thought them of too much value to be stifled, and advised the printing of them. Mr. Collinson then gave them to Cave for publication in his *Gentleman's Magazine*; but he chose to print them separately in a pamphlet, and Dr. Fothergill wrote the preface. Cave, it seems, judged rightly for his profession, for by the additions, that arrived afterwards, they swelled to a quarto volume; which has had five editions, and cost him nothing for copy-money.

It was, however, some time before those papers were much taken notice of in England. A copy of them happening to fall into the hands of the Count de Buffon, a philosopher, deservedly of great reputation in France, and indeed all over Europe, he prevailed with M. Dubourg to translate them into French; and they were printed at Paris. The publication offended the Abbé Nollet, Preceptor in Natural Philosophy to the Royal Family, and an able experimenter, who had formed and published a theory of electricity, which then had the general vogue. He could not at first believe, that such a work came from America, and said it must have been fabricated by his enemies at Paris, to oppose his system. Afterwards, having been assured, that there really existed such a person as Franklin at Philadelphia, which he had doubted, he wrote and published a volume of Letters, chiefly addressed to me, defending his theory, and denying the verity of my experiments, and of the positions deduced from them.

I once purposed answering the Abbé, and actually began the answer; but, on consideration that my writings contained a description of experiments, which any one might repeat and verify, and, if not to be verified, could not be defended: or of observations offered as *conjectures*, and not delivered dogmatically, therefore not laying me under any obligation to defend them; and reflecting, that a dispute between two persons, written in different languages, might be lengthened greatly by mistranslations, and thence misconceptions of one another's meaning, much of one of the Abbé's letters being founded on an error in the translation, I concluded to let my papers shift for themselves; believing it was better to spend what time I could spare from public business in making new experiments, than in disputing about those already made. I therefore never answered M. Nollet; and the event gave me no cause to repent my silence; for my friend M. Le Roy, of the Royal Academy of Sciences, took up my cause and refuted him; my book was translated into the Italian, German, and Latin languages; and the doctrine it contained was by degrees generally adopted by the philosophers of Europe, in preference to that of the Abbé; so that he lived to see himself the last of his sect, except Monsieur B——, of Paris, his *élève* and immediate disciple.

What gave my book the more sudden and general celebrity, was the success of one of its proposed experiments, made by Messieurs Dalibard and De Lor at Marley, for drawing lightning from the clouds. This engaged the public attention everywhere. M. De Lor, who had an apparatus for experimental philosophy, and lectured in that branch of science, undertook to repeat what he called the *Philadelphia Experiments;* and, after they were performed before the King and court, all the curious of Paris flocked to see them. I will not swell this narrative with an account of that capital experiment, nor of the infinite pleasure I received in the success of a similar one I made soon after with a kite at Philadelphia, as both are to be found in the histories of electricity.

Dr. Wright, an English physician, when at Paris, wrote to a friend, who was of the Royal Society, an account of the high esteem my experiments were in among the learned abroad, and of their wonder, that my writings had been so little noticed in England. The Society on this resumed the consideration of the letters that had been read to them; and the celebrated Dr. Watson drew up a summary account of them, and of all I had afterwards sent to England on the subject; which he accompanied with some praise of the writer. This summary was then printed in their *Transactions;* and, some members of the Society in London, particularly the very ingenious Mr. Canton, having verified the experiment of procuring lightning from the clouds by a pointed rod, and acquainted them with the success, they soon made me more than amends for the slight with which they had before treated me. Without my having made any application for that honour, they chose me a member; and voted, that I should be excused the customary payments, which would have amounted to twenty-five guineas; and ever since have given me their *Transactions* gratis.* They also pre-

* Dr. Franklin gives a further account of his election, in a letter to his son, Governor Franklin, from which the following is an extract:—

L

sented me with the gold medal of Sir Godfrey Copley, for
the year 1753, the delivery of which was accompanied by
a very handsome speech of the president, Lord Macclesfield,
wherein I was highly honoured.

CHAPTER XII.

OUR new governor, Captain Denny, brought over for me
the before-mentioned medal from the Royal Society, which he
presented to me at an entertainment given him by the city.
He accompanied it with very polite expressions of his esteem
for me, having, as he said, been long acquainted with my
character.   After dinner, when the company, as was customary at that time, were engaged in drinking, he took me aside
into another room, and acquainted me, that he had been
advised by his friends in England to cultivate a friendship

"London, 19 December, 1767.

"We have had an ugly affair at the Royal Society lately. One Da-
costa, a Jew, who, as our clerk, was intrusted with collecting our
moneys, has been so unfaithful as to embezzle near thirteen hundred
pounds in four years. Being one of the Council this year, as well as
the last, I have been employed all the last week in attending the inquiry into, and unravelling, his accounts, in order to come at a full
knowledge of his frauds. His securities are bound in one thousand
pounds to the Society, which they will pay, but we shall probably lose
the rest. He had this year received twenty-six admission payments of
twenty-five guineas each, which he did not bring to account.
"While attending to this affair, I had an opportunity of looking over
the old council-books and journals of the Society, and, having a curiosity
to see how I came in, of which I had never been informed, I looked
back for the minutes relating to it. You must know, it is not usual to
admit persons that have not requested to be admitted ; and a recommendatory certificate in favour of the candidate, signed by at least three
of the members, is by our rule to be presented to the Society, expressing
that he is desirous of that honour, and is so and so qualified. As I
never had asked, or expected the honour, I was, as I said before, curious
to see how the business was managed. I found that the certificate,
worded very advantageously for me, was signed by Lord Macclesfield,
then President, Lord Parker, and Lord Willoughby; that the election
was by a unanimous vote; and, the honour being voluntarily conferred by
the Society, unsolicited by me, it was thought wrong to demand or receive the usual fees or composition ; so that my name was entered on
the list with a vote of council, *that I was not to pay anything*. And,
accordingly nothing has ever been demanded of me. Those who are
admitted in the common way, pay five guineas admission fees, and two
guineas and a half yearly contributions, or twenty-five guineas down, in
lieu of it. In my case a substantial favour accompanied the honour."—
W. T. F.

with me, as one who was capable of giving him the best advice, and of contributing most effectually to the making his administration easy. That he therefore desired of all things to have a good understanding with me, and he begged me to be assured of his readiness on all occasions to render me every service that might be in his power. He said much to me also of the Proprietor's good disposition towards the province, and of the advantage it would be to us all, and to me in particular, if the opposition that had been so long continued to his measures was dropped, and harmony restored between him and the people; in effecting which it was thought no one could be more serviceable than myself; and I might depend on adequate acknowledgments and recompenses. The drinkers, finding we did not return immediately to the table, sent us a decanter of Madeira, which the Governor made a liberal use of, and in proportion became more profuse of his solicitations and promises.

My answers were to this purpose; that my circumstances, thanks to God, were such as to make Proprietary favours unnecessary to me; and that, being a member of the Assembly, I could not possibly accept of any; that, however, I had no personal enmity to the Proprietary, and that, whenever the public measures he proposed should appear to be for the good of the people, no one would espouse and forward them more zealously than myself; my past opposition having been founded on this, that the measures which had been urged were evidently intended to serve the Proprietary interest, with great prejudice to that of the people. That I was much obliged to him (the Governor) for his profession of regard to me, and that he might rely on everything in my power to render his administration as easy to him as possible, hoping, at the same time, that he had not brought with him the same unfortunate instructions his predecessors had been hampered with.

On this he did not then explain himself; but when he afterwards came to do business with the Assembly, they appeared again, the disputes were renewed, and I was as active as ever in the opposition, being the penman, first of the request to have a communication of the instructions, and then of the remarks upon them, which may be found in the Votes of the times, and in the *Historical Review* I afterwards published. But between us personally no enmity arose; we were often together; he was a man of letters, had seen much of the world, and was entertaining and pleasing in conversation. He gave me information, that my old friend Ralph was still alive: that he was esteemed one of the best political writers in England; had been employed in the dispute between Prince Frederick and the King, and had obtained a pension of three hundred pounds a-year; that his reputation was indeed small as a poet, Pope having damned his poetry in the Dunciad; but his prose was thought as good as any man's.

The Assembly finally finding the Proprietary obstinately persisted in shackling the deputies with instructions inconsistent not only with the privileges of the people, but with the service of the crown, resolved to petition the King against them, and appointed me their agent to go over to England, to present and support the petition. The House had sent up a bill to the Governor, granting a sum of sixty thousand pounds for the King's use, (ten thousand pounds of which was subjected to the orders of the then General, Lord Loudoun,) which the Governor, in compliance with his instructions, absolutely refused to pass.

I had agreed with Captain Morris, of the packet at New York, for my passage, and my stores were put on board; when Lord Loudoun arrived at Philadelphia, expressly, as he told me, to endeavour an accommodation between the Governor and Assembly, that His Majesty's service might not be obstructed by their dissensions. Accordingly he desired the Governor and myself to meet him, that he might hear what was to be said on both sides. We met and discussed the business. In behalf of the Assembly, I urged the various arguments, that may be found in the public papers of that time, which were of my writing, and are printed with the minutes of the Assembly; and the Governor pleaded his instructions, the bond he had given to observe them, and his ruin if he disobeyed; yet seemed not unwilling to hazard himself, if Lord Loudoun would advise it. This his Lordship did not choose to do, though I once thought I had nearly prevailed with him to do it; but finally he rather chose to urge the compliance of the Assembly; and he entreated me to use my endeavours with them for that purpose, declaring that he would spare none of the King's troops for the defence of our frontiers, and that, if we did not continue to provide for that defence ourselves, they must remain exposed to the enemy.

I acquainted the House with what had passed, and—presenting them with a set of resolutions I had drawn up, declaring our rights, that we did not relinquish our claim to those rights, but only suspended the exercise of them on this occasion through *force*, against which we protested—they at length agreed to drop that bill, and frame another conformable to the Proprietary instructions. This of course the Governor passed, and I was then at liberty to proceed on my voyage. But in the meantime the packet had sailed with my sea-stores, which was some loss to me, and my only recompense was his Lordship's thanks for my service; all the credit of obtaining the accommodation falling to his share.

He set out for New York before me; and, as the time for despatching the packet-boats was at his disposition, and there were two then remaining there, one of which, he said, was to sail very soon, I requested to know the precise time, that I might not miss her by any delay of mine. The answer was: " I have given out that she is to sail on Saturday next; but I may let you know, *entre nous*, that if you are there by Monday morning, you will be in time, but do not delay longer." By some accidental hindrance at a ferry, it was Monday noon before I arrived, and I was much afraid she might have sailed, as the wind was fair; but I was soon made easy by the information that she was still in the harbour, and would not move till the next day. One would imagine that I was now on the very point of departing for Europe. I thought so; but I was not then so well acquainted with his Lordship's character, of which *indecision* was one of the strongest features. I shall give some instances. It was about the beginning of April that I came to New York, and I think it was near the end of June before we sailed. There were then two of the packet-boats, which had been long in readiness, but were detained for the General's letters, which were always to be ready *to-morrow*. Another packet arrived; she too was detained; and, before we sailed, a fourth was expected. Ours was the first to be despatched, as having been there longest. Passengers were engaged for all, and some extremely impatient to be gone, and the merchants uneasy about their letters, and for the orders they had given for insurance (it being war time), and for autumnal goods; but their anxiety availed nothing; his Lordship's letters were not ready; and yet whoever waited on him found him always at his desk, pen in hand, and concluded he must needs write abundantly.

Going myself one morning to pay my respects, I found in his antechamber one Innis, a messenger of Philadelphia, who had come thence express, with a packet from Governor Denny for the General. He delivered to me some letters from my friends there, which occasioned my inquiring when he was to return, and where he lodged, that I might send some letters by him. He told me he was ordered to call to-morrow at nine for the General's answer to the Governor, and should set off immediately. I put my letters into his hands the same day. A fortnight after I met him again in the same place. "So, you are soon returned, Innis?" "Returned! no, I am not gone yet." "How so?" "I have called here this and every morning these two weeks past for his Lordship's letters, and they are not yet ready." "Is it possible, when he is so great a writer? for I see him constantly at his escrutoire." "Yes," said Innis, "but he is like St. George on the signs, *always on horseback, and never rides on.*" This observation of the messenger was, it seems, well founded; for, when in England, I understood that Mr. Pitt, afterwards Lord Chatham, gave it as one reason for removing this general, and sending Generals Amherst and Wolfe, *that the minister never heard from him, and could not know what he was doing.*

In this daily expectation of sailing, and all the three packets going down to Sandy Hook, to join the fleet there, the passengers thought it best to be on board, lest by a sudden order the ships should sail, and they be left behind. There, if I remember, we were about six weeks, consuming our sea-stores, and obliged to procure more. At length the fleet sailed, the General and all his army on board, bound to Louisbourg, with intent to besiege and take that fortress; and all the packet-boats in company were ordered to attend the General's ship, ready to receive his despatches when they should be ready. We were out five days before we got a letter with leave to part, and then our ship quitted the fleet and steered for England. The other two packets he still detained, carried them with him to Halifax, where he stayed some time to exercise the men in sham attacks upon sham forts, then altered his mind as to besieging Louisbourg, and returned to New York, with all his troops, together with the two packets above mentioned, and all their passengers! During his absence the French and savages had taken Fort George, on the frontier of that province, and the Indians had massacred many of the garrison after capitulation.

On the whole, I wondered much how such a man came to be intrusted with so important a business, as the conduct of a great army; but, having since seen more of the great world, and the means of obtaining, and motives for giving, places and employments, my wonder is diminished. General Shirley, on whom the command of the army devolved upon the death of Braddock, would, in my opinion, if continued in place, have made a much better campaign than that of Loudoun in 1756, which was frivolous, expensive, and disgraceful to our nation beyond conception. For though Shirley was not bred a soldier, he was sensible and sagacious in himself, and attentive to good advice from others, capable of forming judicious plans, and quick and active in carrying them into execution. Loudoun, instead of defending the colonies with his great army, left them totally exposed, while he paraded idly at Halifax, by which means Fort George was lost; besides he deranged all our mercantile operations, and distressed our trade, by a long embargo on the exportation of provisions, on pretence of keeping supplies from being obtained by the enemy, but in reality for beating down their price in favour of the contractors, in whose profits it was said, perhaps from suspicion only, he had a share; and, when at length the embargo was taken off, neglecting to send notice of it to Charleston, where the Carolina fleet was detained near three months, and whereby their bottoms were so much damaged by the worm, that a great part of them foundered in their passage home.

Shirley was, I believe, sincerely glad of being relieved from so burdensome a charge, as the conduct of an army must be to a man unacquainted with military business. I was at the entertainment given by the city of New York to Lord Loudoun, on his taking upon him the command. Shirley, though thereby superseded, was present also. There was a great company of officers, citizens, and strangers, and, some chairs having been borrowed in the neighbourhood, there was one among them very low, which fell to the lot of Mr. Shirley. I sat by him, and perceiving it, I said, "They have given you a very low seat." "No matter, Mr. Franklin," said he, "I find *a low seat* the easiest."

While I was, as before mentioned, detained at New York, I received all the accounts of the provisions, &c., that I had furnished to Braddock, some of which accounts could not sooner be obtained from the different persons I had employed to assist in the business. I presented them to Lord Loudoun, desiring to be paid the balance. He caused them to be examined by the proper officer, who, after comparing

every article with its voucher, certified them to be right; and
his Lordship promised to give me an order on the paymaster
for the balance due to me. This was, however, put off from
time to time; and, though I called often for it by appointment, I did not get it. At length, just before my departure,
he told me he had, on better consideration, concluded not to
mix his accounts with those of his predecessors. " And you,"
said he, " when in England, have only to exhibit your accounts to the treasury, and you will be paid immediately."

I mentioned, but without effect, a great and unexpected
expense I had been put to by being detained so long at
New York, as a reason for my desiring to be presently paid;
and, on my observing, that it was not right I should be put
to any further trouble or delay in obtaining the money I had
advanced, as I charged no commission for my service, " Oh,"
said he, " you must not think of persuading us, that you are
no gainer; we understand better those matters, and know,
that every one concerned in supplying the army finds means,
in the doing it, to fill his own pockets." I assured him, that
was not my case, and that I had not pocketed a farthing; but
he appeared clearly not to believe me; and indeed I afterwards learned, that immense fortunes are often made in such
employments. As to my balance, I am not paid it to this
day; of which more hereafter.

Our captain of the packet boasted much, before we sailed,
of the swiftness of his ship; unfortunately, when we came to
sea, she proved the dullest of ninety-six sail, to his no small
mortification. After many conjectures respecting the cause,
when we were near another ship almost as dull as ours, which,
however, gained upon us, the captain ordered all hands to
come aft and stand as near the ensign staff as possible. We
were, passengers included, about forty persons. While we
stood there, the ship mended her pace, and soon left her
neighbour far behind, which proved clearly what our captain
suspected, that she was loaded too much by the head. The
casks of water, it seems, had been all placed forward; these
he therefore ordered to be moved further aft, on which the
ship recovered her character, and proved the best sailer in the
fleet.

The foregoing fact I give for the sake of the following observation. It has been remarked, as an imperfection in the
art of ship-building, that it can never be known till she is
tried, whether a new ship will, or will not, be a good sailer;

for that the model of a good-sailing ship has been exactly followed in a new one, which has been proved on the contrary remarkably dull. I apprehend, that this may partly be occasioned by the different opinions of seamen respecting the modes of loading, rigging, and sailing of a ship; each has his method; and the same vessel, laden by the method and orders of one captain, shall sail worse than when by the orders of another. Besides, it scarce ever happens, that a ship is formed, fitted for the sea, and sailed by the same person. One man builds the hull, another rigs her, a third loads and sails her. No one of these has the advantage of knowing all the ideas and experience of the others, and, therefore, cannot draw just conclusions from a combination of the whole.

Even in the simple operation of sailing when at sea, I have often observed different judgments in the officers, who commanded the successive watches, the wind being the same. One would have the sails trimmed sharper or flatter than another, so that they seemed to have no certain rule to govern by. Yet I think a set of experiments might be instituted, first, to determine the most proper form of the hull for swift sailing; next, the best dimensions and most proper place for the masts; then the form and quantity of sails, and their position, as the winds may be; and lastly, the disposition of the lading. This is an age of experiments, and I think a set accurately made and combined would be of great use.

We were several times chased in our passage, but outsailed everything; and in thirty days had soundings. We had a good observation, and the captain judged himself so near our port, Falmouth, that, if we made a good run in the night, we might be off the mouth of that harbour in the morning; and by running in the night might escape the notice of the enemy's privateers, who often cruised near the entrance of the Channel. Accordingly all the sail was set that we could possibly carry, and the wind being very fresh and fair, we stood right before it, and made great way. The captain, after his observation, shaped his course, as he thought, so as to pass wide of the Scilly Rocks; but it seems there is sometimes a strong current setting up St. George's Channel, which formerly caused the loss of Sir Cloudesley Shovel's squadron, in 1707. This was probably also the cause of what happened to us.

We had a watchman placed in the bow, to whom they often called, "*Look well out before there:*" and he as often answered "*Ay, ay;*" but perhaps had his eyes shut, and was half asleep at the time; they sometimes answering, as is said, mechanically: for he did not see a light just before us, which had been hid by the studding-sails from the man at the helm, and from the rest of the watch, but by an accidental yaw of the ship was discovered, and occasioned a great alarm, we being very near it; the light appearing to me as large as a cart-wheel. It was midnight, and our captain fast asleep; but Captain Kennedy, jumping upon deck, and seeing the danger, ordered the ship to wear round, all sails standing; an operation dangerous to the masts, but it carried us clear, and we avoided shipwreck. for we were running fast on the rocks, on which the light was erected. This deliverance impressed me strongly with the utility of lighthouses, and made me resolve to encourage the building some of them in America, if I should live to return thither.

In the morning it was found by the soundings that we were near our port, but a thick fog hid the land from our sight. About nine o'clock the fog began to rise, and seemed to be lifted up from the water like the curtain of a theatre, discovering underneath the town of Falmouth, the vessels in the harbour, and the fields that surround it. This was a pleasing spectacle to those, who had been long without any other prospect than the uniform view of a vacant ocean, and it gave us the more pleasure, as we were now free from the anxieties which had arisen.*

I set out immediately, with my son, for London, and we only stopped a little by the way to view Stonehenge on Salisbury Plain, and Lord Pembroke's house and gardens, with the very curious antiquities, at Wilton. We arrived in London, the 27th of July, 1757.†

* In a letter from Dr. Franklin to his wife, dated at Falmouth, the 17th of July, 1757, after giving her a similar account of his voyage, escape, and landing, he adds; "The bell ringing for church, we went thither immediately, and, with hearts full of gratitude, returned sincere thanks to God for the mercies we had received. Were I a Roman Catholic, perhaps I should on this occasion vow to build a chapel to some saint; but as I am not, if I were to vow at all, it should be to build a *lighthouse.*"—W. T. F.

† Here close Dr. Franklin's Memoirs, as written by himself. From several passages in his letters it would seem, that it was his intention to continue them further, and perhaps to the end of his life; but public business for some time, and afterwards his declining health, prevented him from executing his purpose.—ED.